SUCCUBUS CHAINED

SHACKLED SOULS 1

HEATHER LONG

PARANORMAL
PRISON

Welcome to Nightmare Penitentiary

Siren Condemned by C.R. Jane and Mila Young
Delinquent Demons by K. Webster
Conveniently Convicted by Raven Kennedy & Ivy Asher
Noir Reformatory by Lexi C. Foss & Jennifer Thorn
Blindly Indicted by Katie May
Wraith Captive by Lacey Carter Andersen
Stolen Song by Autumn Reed & Ripley Proserpina
Prison Princess by CoraLee June & Rebecca Royce
Succubus Chained by Heather Long
Siren Sacrificed by C.R. Jane & Mila Young
Succubus Unchained by Heather Long

SUCCUBUS CHAINED

SHACKLED SOULS BOOK 1

Nightmare Penitentiary

I bet you're asking yourself, why am I here? What happened that landed me in this cell? Trust me, you aren't the only one.

Who am I?

You'd do better to ask what I am.

You know it's going to be a bad day when you wake up in the wrong man's bed, your favorite leather outfit is completely shredded, your best Manolo Blahniks are broken, and your eighty-dollar manicure is ruined.

But would you believe me if I said that's just the tip of the shit storm?

My name is Fiona MacRieve, and I'm a succubus...or I was. I seduced a vampire and we had a fantastic time, until he drained me almost to death. Which wouldn't have been so bad if he hadn't forced his blood down my throat thinking it would heal me.

Yeah, it didn't.

Cause that's not how I heal.

So not only did I wake up to losing my best outfit, I woke up dead.

Now I'm a vampire.

Some shit you just can't make up.

Oh…and my favorite part? I'm under arrest.

FOREWORD & DEDICATION

First, I'd like to say thank you for picking up Succubus Chained and giving this tale a shot. When invited to join this collection of paranormal prison tales, I immediately thought back to a blurb I'd written five or six years ago.

The tale of a succubus inadvertently turned into a vampire. I've wanted to write this book for *years*, but it never seemed the right time. Now I know why. Fiona wanted to wait for this moment, this setting, this story and I'm thrilled to be able to share this scorching hot tale.

Fair warning, this book is probably hotter than any I've ever written and the heroes are downright swoon worthy. I'd like to take a moment to thank C.R. Jane, Mila Young, Rebecca Royce, Lexi Foss, Lacey Carter Andersen, Ripley Proserpina, Autumn Reed, Katie May, K. Webster, Jennifer Thorn, Coralee June, Ivy Asher, and Raven Kennedy. These amazing authors have been a blast to share this journey with. Also hats off to my pack, Lysanne Therrien, Blake Blessing (who kept changing her mind on who her favorite hero was) and Sara Vermillion. You all rock!

Finally, just a couple of housekeeping notes!

For those of you who have never read a reverse harem before, thanks for picking this up and giving it a shot. A reverse harem means the heroine will not make a choice in this book or any other between the guys in her life. It may take her a while to reach that conclusion, but it's the journey that drives it. There are many ways to frame this kind of relationship, currently reverse harem fits it very well.

While there may be no specific happy endings at the end of each of these books, there will be one to the whole trilogy, that I promise you. Some of these books will have cliffhangers, largely due to the size of the story, but the happy ending has to be earned as part of the journey.

Thank you again for reading Fiona's story and I truly hope you enjoy it!

Warning, this book contains aggressively snarky characters, a bit of twisted humor and a lot of passion.

— HEATHER LONG

CHAPTER 1

"Of all the things you choose in life, you don't get to choose what your nightmares are. You don't pick them; they pick you" - John Irving

I didn't want to be a damn vampire. The screams echoed off the stone. The sound distant, yet anguished. It must be that time. In the two weeks since I'd been dumped into this place, I'd tracked the routine by when those screams began.

It marked the death and birth of a new day. The chill in the room barely touched me. I wouldn't have minded better accommodations. Despite my expensive tastes, the damp, stone cell with its single hard bed, a sink that allowed water for washing, and a toilet in the corner they'd actually let me clean before I touched it—look, a girl has to have some standards—was empty.

I was also the only one in this wing, so the wrought iron door, reinforced with its magical protections and salted to boot, didn't even provide me a view of the emptiness beyond. It was all shadows. The sconces in the corners lit up in the "morning" and extinguished at "night."

I'd destroyed them twice.

The little bastards always popped back up.

Still, it was something to do when the mental retail therapy grew stale. Currently, I debated between a pair of Louboutins that were last season and the Stuart Weitzman that were just perfectly classic and provocative. Both had stellar heels and would definitely work for my ass. The red-bottomed Louboutins had gotten a little too common. Everyone wanted to be seen in them.

The screams climbed in volume. It would be nice if he could arrive without the serenade. The noise was hardly conducive to mood.

Still, if I went for the Weitzman, what would I pair them with? I was still mentally scrolling through the dress racks when I considered ditching the heels for thigh high boots and a mini-skirt. I had fabulously long legs, and I knew how to work them. Thigh highs screamed 'come and get me.'

Heat and hunger vied for my attention as I shifted on the bed. The problem was that my fabulously toned legs were looking a little too slender. The thigh highs would hide the loss of tone.

Thigh highs it was.

The door grated open, and I didn't bother rising as he suddenly filled the space. The shadows deepened, darkening the already pitch space. Seeing in the dark had never been my talent, yet I could make him out as easily as if the sconces were lit. Tall, rangy, and gorgeous, despite the mean streak in him.

"Fiona," he greeted me as he closed the door and made his way across the cell. Not like he had far to travel.

"Dorran," I mocked his deep, husky tone as I crossed one

leg over the other. I wore the equivalent of a polyester jump suit in the most horrid shade of gray. The color was so drab, it blended with the walls around me.

Chuckling, he held out a hand as he stood in front of me. "You haven't been eating."

I rolled my eyes and ignored his hand. "I don't survive on blood."

"You used to not need it," he reminded me, as if I could forget. Even the mention of it had my teeth sharpening. The canines weren't quite as pronounced as most vampires. I hadn't been born one or even turned like they sometimes chose with the human cattle they kept close to them. I certainly shouldn't be one now.

Stupid. Fucking. Dimitri.

When I got out of here—and I would—I planned to gut Dimitri and hang him by his entrails. When he healed, I'd do it again.

A few centuries of that, and I might be willing to let bygones be bygones, or simply rip his head totally off.

That would be nice.

The lust for blood sent another wave of heat and hunger to balloon through me. It didn't help to have him looming over me, flushed with a lust of his own, and it wasn't just lust for me, though that was definitely present. Dorran had been feeding, and it practically coiled around him, a dark energy that licked at my skin, even if he wasn't touching me.

Demons, after all, understood other demons.

With a growl, he clasped my hand and yanked me to my feet. The moment his mouth crashed down on mine, I gave in to the need to feed. Blood may be among my cravings now, but it wasn't what I needed to survive.

With hot heavy hands, he shoved up my top, even as I pulled at his vestments. His tongue tangled with mine, and he tasted of coffee, cake, and passion. Someone had been dining well this evening. When he pulled back to yank my shirt up and over, I got his jacket off.

The clothes hit the floor with a thump. Other prisoners might try to purloin something from his pockets or steal from him. I wanted what was under the clothes. The power eddying over his skin stroked mine, and the shadows began to sink into me before he looped an arm around my bare waist and dragged me back.

Mouth on mine, he began to feast. The despair and aggravation in my blood churned as he sought to suck it out of me. Fisting his hair, I hiked my thighs to his hips. He had one hand on my ass, lifting me, and I began to writhe against the hard length of cock pressed right against my pussy.

Fuck, his lust magnified. Even as he dragged the despair out of me, I began to feast on the hunger in him. It was a magnificent loop.

After four days of denying him, I was starved for it. He drove me back against the wall, and I fisted him into position. The rough stone scraped at my back. Without waiting or warning, he slammed into me. Eyes rolling back, I tipped my head away. The pistoning of his hips jolted me right between pleasure and pain, a seesawing effect that only heightened his wanton desire.

When he bit against my throat, I bucked back at him. Fucker loved to mark me, even if he didn't require blood. The thrust of darkness teased against my anus. It was his turn to fist my hair, and he dragged my gaze to him.

A scream broke free as he began to prod the tight rosette, his lust magnified, and a choked laugh broke out of me.

"It's that or you feed on blood," he ordered me, and his whole body vibrated against mine. Not once did he stop drilling into me. My breasts scrapped against the sweaty heat of his chest, the hairs there prickling my nipples. His power thickened as he began to breach the puckered opening, and another shudder raced through me.

He wanted me so bad, and it flooded my starved senses.

"Fiona," he snarled my name, and I clenched my teeth in a grimace as his thrusts grew more ferocious. Every glorious slam he ground against my clit. The hot slide of his cock through me only ratcheted the temperature in my body higher. My blood thundered as his lust filled me.

"You want me," I snarled at him, digging my nails into his bare shoulders. "Then take it."

The flare of surprise followed by a swelling in both in his cock and his need threatened to tip me over. The shadows went hazy as he pummeled me, and my parched soul soaked up every drop. The first thrust of shadows filling my anus sent pain splintering through the pleasure, and he lapped it up even as he stilled his thrusting. Impaled on both his body and his power, I met his gaze. Heat roiled around me, in me, and him.

A testing probe, he eased the shadow thrust back and slammed his cock into me.

Fuck.

I forgot how to speak as he began to drive all thoughts from my head.

"That's it." He ground out the words somehow as he ramped his pace up. Every thrust of him stretched me. What pain his abrupt penetration caused faded as his lust spilled over onto everything. He could have carved me up right now, and I'd have orgasmed from the knife.

The scent of copper flickered across my drunken mind, and then he had my face pressed against his throat, and the first sticky drops hit my tongue. Instinct had me sinking my teeth in.

The hot flow of blood hit my mouth, rich in spice and power. The first gulp was like ice-cold water in the boiling desert. It made me desperate for more. As soon as I latched on, he began to rock his hips again. Thrust, counterthrust, he kept my body full as I gluttoned on his lust and blood.

When he began to nail that sweet spot with every hammer home, I screamed against his throat but I kept drinking. I needed it so bad. I needed everything he had, and he let out a roar as he came. We leaned there, him buried in me and panting as he emptied himself, and I kept lapping at his throat, wanting more of the power rich blood.

Gradually, the tension of his hand lighting my scalp up as he tugged on my hair pulled me free from feeding, and I met his gleaming gaze a split second before his smirking mouth closed over mine.

Too drunk to care, I cradled him and let him hold me against the wall until his cock finally slipped free. He didn't knot, but it took him time after release to soften enough to leave me.

Then he turned me from the wall and dropped me on the bed. Naked. Spent. And floating on a haze of it.

"Do not wait so long next time," he told me as he drew a finger down my cheek to my breast. "You are not dying on my watch, Fiona."

The possession in his voice should worry me, but fuck, it would hardly be the first time a lover—even one as casual as he was—decided I was something to be collected. Part of the reason I was stuck here in the first place.

"Fuck you, Dorran," I managed to slur. Why did he have to taste so good? I hated the need for blood, and it was that loathing that he began to soak up as he knelt down and latched his mouth over a nipple. Instead of pushing him away, I gripped his head and kept him there, until his shadows thrust into my pussy this time and tumbled me over the precipice into a deep, drunken stupor.

Nothing left of me to worry about.

It was the only reason I had to have imagined him smoothing the sweat-dampened hair from my face and the almost chaste kiss he left on my forehead.

"When I send you blood tomorrow," he whispered at my ear. "You will drink."

In my dream, I flipped him off, but he'd already pulled on his clothes after folding mine neatly and setting them at the foot of the bed. Then the warden was gone. I didn't even hear the rattle and slam of the door.

The screams continued after that, but I drifted on a lazy river of sensation. I barely twitched when the sconces lit, marking a new day. Replete and flushed with energy and vigor, I was like a cat who wanted to stretch out in the sun.

Except there was no sun.

And I was still in prison for the crime of being impossible.

I was a succubus, but a vampire turned me after he drained me to the point of death.

Idiot.

When I woke, I was living yet not. I was a succubus, yet also a vampire. My favorite outfit had been trashed, and my best shoes broken. My creator also panicked and fled, sticking me with the hotel room bill.

Do you have any idea what it costs to clean blood out of carpet?

Worse still, when I went to the city's vampires for some assistance in finding the asshat who'd fucked up my life, I ended up here.

In prison.

Yep.

So if you wanted to know how I got here, that's it.

For the last two weeks, these four stone walls have housed me and the warden—he told me to call him Dorran—

has been my only visitor. He wants me to feed. But I don't survive on blood alone.

I wish I didn't need the blood at all.

Four times now, he's had to force the issue.

Totally worth it by the way, because I won't touch that bagged stuff, and if the only way to feed my lust was to get him to show up, then I still wouldn't touch the bags.

I shifted against the bed, aware of every scratchy inch of the blanket and the uncomfortable, almost slab-like surface the too thin mattress covered. Nothing else here offered even a little bit of pleasure. Dorran, on the other hand, definitely filled a need.

Lazing through the day, I barely rose by evening to clean myself up at the sink and to get some water to drink. I could actually eat real food, not that they brought me any.

When the bags of blood arrived through the slot in the door, I was already back to leaning against my wall, dressed in the drab gray with my damp hair drying slowly. At least I could wash.

Instead of thigh-high boots, I decided I'd shop for jewelry tonight. Even if I was almost full to the brim, I wouldn't be opposed to my sometime visitor.

It gave me something to do while I wasn't allowed to rot away in here.

The funny thing was, if they didn't want the world to know about me, why would they want to keep me alive?

Why not just stake me or burn me alive or something?

Hell, cut off my head. Chop chop, and we're done.

Rolling my eyes, I jerked my attention back to virtual shopping.

My name is Fiona MacRieve. Always good to remember that part.

I was a succubus.

Or I used to be.

Now?

I didn't know what I'd become.

But as long as they planned on keeping me alive, they better hope they could keep me in here, because my lust for vengeance grew by the hour, and I could feed on that, too.

Just saying.

CHAPTER 2

"A lion's work hours are only when he's hungry; once he's satisfied, the predator and prey live peacefully together." - Chuck Jones

$\mathcal{T}$he next week passed much as the first two here had. I'd finally begun to decorate my new vacation house. The one I hadn't purchased yet, but would be on my list when I got out of here. I used to have this really great loft apartment that overlooked a river. Some nights, when there were fireworks, I could lie in bed and watch them go off.

My new place would be high up, too. Something with lots of windows...whether I could take the sun or not was semantics. I hadn't actually tested the theory. I'd pretty much woken up trashed, dead, and sporting some semi-fangs that weren't as nice as those you could buy at a costume shop.

Then I was here.

In this *hole* at the bottom of the world.

Focus. The mental chastisement pulled me back to the target. Cliff house, maybe something sitting up on a bluff. I wanted to look out over the ocean this time, not just a river, and I didn't want city lights in the distance…or did I?

Compromise. Put a secondary deck on the opposite side that would let me look at a city in the distance. That would work, but I wanted my bedroom open to the ocean. I wanted to be able to throw open the windows and let in the breeze. I wanted to taste fresh, salty air and feel the sun warm my skin.

A clang in the hall jerked me out of my building. Irritated, I sat up on the bed as the first clang was followed by a second. Then the unrelenting clanging grew in force and volume. My head began to pulse in time to the banging, and I scowled.

It was too early for Dorran to come calling. He'd only come twice in the last seven days. Both times because I'd refused to feed. The last time had been the night before. My hunger and my body were both well-sated. I usually enjoyed a lovely period of hazy daydreaming in the first couple of days after glutting myself.

As distasteful as drinking blood was, I had begun craving his. Probably why the fresh blood bags they'd delivered at first light still lay right next to the door. I wasn't touching them. I didn't even like how they smelled.

The racket outside increased in volume until it seemed the pound right through my body, splintering any focus I tried to rebuild. Glaring at the door, I waited. *This* was a departure in my routine.

After three weeks of staring at walls punctuated by nightly screaming and the regular visits of the warden for some bouts of fucking and feeding, *this* stood out.

The clanging stopped abruptly a split-second before the metal of my door screeched a complaint when it was hauled open. It didn't open inward, no, that would allow me to block it. It swung out, so they could also barricade me in.

A guard filled the doorway. Well, maybe it was a guard. He was dressed in a heavy black uniform with tight leather breeches that were doing fabulous things for his thighs. His ferocious expression betrayed nothing.

Dude had *mastered* resting dick face.

Awesome.

The piercing frost of his almost silver eyes bored right through me. "Fiona MacRieve?"

Rolling my shoulders back, I gave him a bored look. "Depends."

"On what?" he barked in a growly voice, something like shock creeping across his scruffed face. The straight edged nose above his very full lips added to the overall appeal. He didn't belong in this dark, dank place. The flickering light from the sconces played over his face and warmed him a fraction.

Course, that could just be a trick of the light.

He took a single step inside, but I didn't respond. Instead, I just watched him. The sudden shift in routine offered me an opportunity. The question was what kind opportunity.

"Answer the question, woman," he growled, then his nostrils flared as he studied me. Another deep inhale, and he frowned even deeper.

One moment, he was at the door, and the next, he was in front of me. The flash of movement so swift, I didn't have time to escape before he hauled me up by the arms. "Are you Fiona MacRieve?"

"Well, like I said," I drawled slowly. "That depends on who's asking." Poor fool. This close, I could taste the desire and lust simmering under his fierce exterior. The ice in those eyes cloaked a much deeper fire. The male reminded me of the warden in some ways. Rich, powerful, and intoxicating in his wantonness—funnily enough, it wasn't my body pulling at him at the moment. The lust wasn't physical.

But it was primal.

I could work with that.

Ignoring his bruising grip on my arms, I lifted a hand to test the roughness of his face. "Who are you, sugar?"

His nostrils flared even as his pupils expanded then constricted to pinpricks. That was also different.

And not in a good way.

"Yes, you're her," he answered his own question instead of mine. When he thrust his face at my throat, I slammed my knee up between his very sexy thighs. Those gorgeous leather breeches really did him justice.

Unfortunately—for him anyway—he wasn't wearing a cup. Across nearly all creatures shadowy and otherwise, the male of the species was very vulnerable to attacks on their genitals, provoked or not.

Though, arguably, if someone slammed their leg up against my pussy like that, I would be in similar pain. His grimace at the blow promised me I'd landed it true, but he didn't release me.

I repeated the gesture, and this time, I slammed my head forward at the same time. That beautiful nose I'd been admiring crunched gorgeously, and his pained gasp accompanied the sudden release of my arms. As he swayed, I shoved him backward. The head butting left me seeing stars, but I'd stumbled out of plenty of bars drunk off my ass riding the lustful wave of humanity, I didn't need to see clearly to move.

Once out in the hall, I swung my gaze left and then right. Fantastic, it was all rough-hewn stone, and both directions looked exactly the same.

Fine, I went right.

I passed by other iron doors, locked and barricaded. I didn't bother to try them. They opened out. The door to get out of here would open also open out, but I would be on the inside of it.

Jogging, I thrilled to the fact Dorran had fed me so well, even if he'd left me sore and achy in all the right ways. But I was full, and I had strength. The hallway seemed to elongate or stretch on to infinity. There were no bends or curves.

That wasn't good. If I couldn't find a corner to turn soon, there was every chance my surprise visitor would catch me up. He definitely had fit and virile going on for him, even if I'd left him breathless and cupping his nuts like a little bitch.

Served him right.

I'd barely found the door I could push outward when the scuff of a step on stone reached my ears.

Dammit.

Risking a magical shock, I shoved the door open. The racket clanged up the hallway. The volume jolted me.

All the doors I'd passed…

Dick boy—fine, man—had opened every door along the hall on his way to me. That explained the clanging racket. Not good. No one had stopped him, that meant the guard had either been dispatched down here to fetch me for something nefarious or more likely to just kill me.

Stumbling out into a stairwell, I growled to myself. The door slammed shut behind me with tremendous force. Yeah, no one would miss the gong of that.

Up?

Down?

Damn good question.

The obvious answer would be up, because I'd been in the pit, right? No windows, sealed inside a stone coffin that just happened to be room-sized. I didn't have time to debate this in a committee of me, myself, and I. I flipped a mental coin.

Fine.

Down it was.

If up was the obvious answer, then down would be the correct route.

Descending the stone steps, I kept close to the wall. The smell of musk grew stronger the lower I went. Wet animals. Maybe dog.

Wolf.

Ugh.

Howling echoed behind the first set of doors I reached. Yeah, not opening the door to find the big, oversized floof-balls who wanted to rip out my throat. Last time I checked, vamps and wolves weren't exactly kissing cousins.

More like spitting, snarling, and teeth gnashing. Though my bestie had been a wolf. Hopefully, he hadn't heard about the latest and greatest. It'd be a real bitch to have to throw down with Elias.

Man could make a smoked brisket better than anyone I'd ever known, and I'd be really pissed if I never got invited over for dinner anymore. Continuing the downward trajectory, I listened for the raucous noise of the door opening above. Hopefully, when dick man got there, he'd go up.

Up made sense.

Why the fuck had I thought going down made more sense?

It was three more flights before I found another door of any kind. Was I about to knock on Hell's back door?

Like the door from my floor to the stairwell, this one opened away from the hall. I extended a hand to test the magical protections. I was on the outside, so they should be geared toward keeping stuff in, not out?

Then again, I went down—look, it seemed reasonable at the time, and I might still be a little drunk on Dorran—so what did I know?

Energy licked against my fingers, and the vaguest of hums

touched my ears. Dammit. Definitely warded. Warded to what? Give a sweet tickle, or blow someone's head off?

Last I checked, those spells were actually in the same category. Don't look at me like that, succubus here, not a witch. They do some messed up stuff.

A hush of breath was my only warning before powerful hands seized me, hauled me backward, and slammed me against the wall.

"Oh," I drawled after I caught my breath again. Having it all knocked out of me was a point in my favor. Fucking vampires didn't need to breathe. I did.

Score one for me. Take that you twisted fucks.

Still, I stared up at the now bloodied face of my erstwhile visitor and his very, excuse me, extremely pissed off face. Resting dick face had taken active to a whole new level.

"You are a pain in the ass," he snarled.

"Look who's talking, jackass," I retorted. "I was minding my own business in that cell when you got all handsy." For evidence I glanced at those huge paws he called hands currently pinning me to the wall. In fact, most of him was pinning me to the wall, and it was hot.

His lustful fragrance swarmed me, and I wanted to take hits off of it. I might need the extra boost, but I didn't need to go into a stupor, so I kept it to the mouth breathing.

For. The. Moment.

"Why do you smell like a man?"

"Because you're a little whacked. Trust me, no penis here. Currrently."

I smirked at my response.

"Need to check?" I widened my stance a little. It took some wiggling, but it ground me against him and the now very thick evidence of *his* penis. "I can feel yours, seems only fair you check out mine or the lack thereof."

His growl vibrated right through me, and fuck, that felt

good. Okay, first, I didn't need to feed, so stop it. Second, growling boy might want to eat me and not even in a nice way, so *focus.*

Tilting my head to the side, I considered licking him just to see what he would do.

Could be fun.

Might get me killed.

Both were definitely more than I had to do an hour ago.

"Also, kudos for the erection, man. I was pretty sure two slams of my knee would have knocked your balls into your throat."

Poor baby was not amused.

"Who touched you?" Each word came out on a spikey, near guttural sound, swallowing the vowels.

Kind of sexy in a primitive caveman way.

"At the moment, hot stuff, that would be you."

He shook me once. This close to the wall, it only served to knock my skull against the stone. Great, the stars I'd still been seeing since earlier now had do-si-do partners to dance with.

"Who *fucked* you?"

Oh.

That.

"Do you really want to know?" I asked, more curious than anything for his response.

"Yes," he rasped.

"Let's see—that would be 'none' and 'of' along side 'your fucking' and wait for it, 'business.'"

His brows pulled together. "You'll tell me, and I'll deal with it."

"Yeah, okay, this isn't entertaining anymore. We need to communicate in more than grunts." When he pushed his hips at me again, I debated his reaction if I slammed my knee up once more. He was pretty hard. "Thanks for the offer, by the way, I'm not hungry."

A puzzled look crossed his face for a split second, then he did something utterly unexpected.

He laughed. What the fuck?

Before I could verbalize the question, he closed his exceptionally large hand around my throat. While he didn't squeeze, the strength there couldn't be denied. "I wasn't offering you my blood, Fiona," he told me.

"I didn't think you were, since it's all in your cock," I countered.

He snorted. "Thank you for confirming you're Fiona."

"Discussing your dick does not make me Fiona."

Frustration filled his eyes. "Why are you being difficult?"

Was he for real?

"Um...look around," I pointed out. "What do you see?"

"You descending to the darkest parts of the penitentiary, where even the most dangerous hunters would be loathe to go."

"Cool, you run along then." Dammit, I knew I should have gone up.

He let out aggrieved sigh. "Not without you."

"Excuse me?"

"I'm here to rescue you."

Rescue. Me.

"Why the fuck didn't you say that upstairs instead of getting all monosyllabic and snarly?"

"Because you smell like another man, he's been all over you." He tilted my head to the side and then stroked his thumb over my throat. Told you Dorran liked to mark me. "He's done it recently, too. Are you sure you won't tell me who?"

"Nope," I said. "I don't fuck and tell. Rules of the game."

Not really, but I didn't know this guy, and rescue or not, I was not in the mood for this crap.

His lips compressed into a thin line, and he dropped his hand from my throat. When he backed up a single step and gave me room to breathe, I narrowed my eyes. That was an unexpected twist. Reaching behind him, he pulled out a pair of shackles, and I glared at him.

"No." I was not going in chains.

"You have to," he said. "I'm a guard. I can get you out if I *escort* you. But prisoners are not allowed to roam freely."

"No." I folded my arms. I was not going to put those on willing.

"I will take them off, Fiona. I promise." The growl underscoring each syllable didn't inspire confidence. Besides…

"I don't even know you, why would your promise mean shit to me?"

"My name is Maddox." He intoned it so formally, like I would recognize him by the moniker alone. Was it like Madonna or Cher? If so, 'fraid it was lost on me. "I'm here to see you to safety."

"Define safety," I challenged. "And why I should believe you just because of your name, which for the record, doesn't mean anything to me."

Surprise crystalized in his expression edged by real frustration.

Yeah, I had a gift.

"Woman, I don't care if you believe me. I'll carry you out of here kicking and screaming. I can knock you out if I have to." He dragged my arm out and slammed one of the shackles on. It burned as it snapped around my wrist. "I'm rescuing you whether you want to go or not."

Why the fuck would I not want to go?

I just wanted to know whether I was going somewhere better or not.

He wrestled me into the second shackle, and I let out a frustrated scream as it closed on my free wrist. They were spelled. The magic in them burned where they rested against my flesh. Dick face—Maddox—stared down as my skin began to blister and smoke.

"That should not be happening."

Oh.

That was it.

This guy?

I was killing him first.

Shackled wrists and all, I clenched my fists together and struck both at his bloody nose.

If I didn't break it the first time, I was damn well going to break it now. Unfortunately, he caught the slender chain locking my wrists together and hauled my arms up to slam them against the wall before he boxed me against it again.

"Stop fighting me," he ordered. "The shackles have a spell."

"No shit."

"The spell is to help us get you out."

Us.

Wait.

Gritting my teeth against the blistering sensation crawling over my skin and scalding it, I asked, "Who's us?"

A flash of teeth. "You'll find out. When you come with me."

I hated this man.

Alarms began to sound and doors above opened with a clang. His expression turned furious. When he turned that glare on me, I gave him a little shrug. Or at least, as much as I could manage pinned to the wall in his murder bracelets.

"Oops?"

CHAPTER 3

"The beauty of the soul shines out when a man bears with composure one heavy mischance after another, not because he does not feel them, but because he is a man of high and heroic temper." - Aristotle

Maddox

*I*f he didn't want to kill her, Maddox might end up liking her. As it was, she fought like a hellion, blooded him, and managed to evade him by persistently doing the unexpected. As more doors opened above, he clenched his jaw. Then again, if he managed to get both of them to safety before this was over, he might just kill her himself and to hell with what Fin wanted.

Cutting his attention back to her red and blistering wrists, he ground his teeth together. The wild, erratic path had taken them far from the mapped exit. More guards would be upon them at any minute.

"Take them off," she ordered, and his cock pulsed with

every word spilling from her lips. The fact that she reeked of another male did him no favors. He waxed and waned between homicidal rage that someone had touched her while she'd been trapped here, and the very distinct urge to override that scent with his own.

Neither was useful in their current situation. A situation, he might add, that was her *fault*.

Shooting a look behind him at the door to the unknown level, he gripped the chain between the shackles and tugged her from the wall. Her hiss of pain dragged his attention to the blistered and reddened skin of her wrists. The spelled shackles shouldn't be reacting to either her succubus nature or her vampiric side.

Then again, she was a baby vamp.

Fuck, he'd have to take them off. He didn't want her suffering. Gripping the door, he wrenched it open and glared through the opening. The shadowed hall looked identical to the one he'd pursued her from her cell to the stairwell in the first place.

Fuck Fin and his fired hurry to get in here. They should have tracked her together, gotten her out together.

Better, he should have just let Maddox do it himself. Hunting was his thing. Dragging her with him, he strode down the hall. The sealed cells all looked the same, but the magic on them was different.

Something he'd noticed on her level. The unoccupied cells didn't have a metallic taint to the spell work on the doors. Something charged one of the doors they past and hit it hard enough to shake the whole frame. Magic flared, and yowl pierced the air.

That would probably leave a mark.

"Where are you going?"

"Be quiet," he ordered. The last thing he needed was for

his body and instincts to riot and override his common sense. The urge to strip her naked and sink his teeth into her grew with every passing moment. To his surprise, she cooperated and went silent. Instead of forcing him to drag her, she moved up alongside.

For exactly three more doors, then she clasped his forearm. The weight of her slender fingers gave him little warning for when she twisted the chain from his grasp while wrenching his arm up against his back. She tried to drive him into the wall.

Nice attempt.

Sexy little kitten.

Strong, too.

But he was stronger. He bore back on the force of her arms, not needing the leverage. Her little gasp as he whirled and caught her by the throat as he successfully slammed her against the wall did all sorts of things to his libido.

"Stop fighting me," he ordered. "I don't want to hurt you." Quite the contrary, he wanted to lick her from one end of her body to the other, until he satisfied this wild craving she'd evoked.

"That's not going to happen." The stunning amber of her eyes dared him to retaliate. Most newborns boasted blood-red eyes their first couple of years. Something about the tissue in their body and how it adapted to the need to feed. Barely weeks old, Fiona's eyes were as unique as she was.

Narrowing the distance, he forced himself to breathe through his mouth, though that did little to mute the stench of her lover or her far more provocative nature beneath it. Rage kindled in his blood, racing through his system with claws and teeth. Maddox wouldn't forget that scent. "Fiona," he focused on her eyes as he mouthed her name. *This* particular trick wasn't his specialty. "You have to cooperate until we're secure. Then I'll remove the shackles. Tell me you understand."

She laughed in his face, and Maddox snarled. The beast inside of him lunged forward until they were nose to nose. The humor in her expression drained away, but not the murder she promised him in her eyes.

"You want to kill me, kitten. You're going to have to live long enough to do that. I could snap your neck and leave your corpse here as I made my way out. You'd wake up back in your cell, and you'd never find me."

Her upper lip curled. "Fine," she conceded. "But as long as we're clear on the fact that I am going to fucking kill you."

Maddox snorted, then licked her cheek from the curve of her jaw to the corner of her eye. It was a stupidly possessive and territorial gesture, but he did it anyway. "I'm pretty clear on the facts, kitten," he whispered before jerking her away from the wall and gripping the chain once more.

"Blegh," she grimaced. "Dick."

"You wound me, kitten," he snarked. Braced for any further attempts, he resumed his mad dash to find them a place to ride out the security breach. Twelve doors later, he found what he wanted. Gripping the door, he yanked it open and ignored the racket it made. Just another lovely feature of the supernatural roach motel they called Nightmare Penitentiary.

Empty.

Hauling her inside, he released her in the direction of the empty cot in the corner. This room was actually smaller than the one he'd found her in, but it would do. Pulling the door closed, he put a palm against the handle and muttered three words. Now to see if the cost of those syllables had been worth it. The spells flared, and his nose burned at the sudden icy metallic stink wafting at him. Retreating a few steps, he settled into a stance as he listened.

To his continued surprise, Fiona didn't interrupt or say a word. It wasn't long before the shuffle of footsteps reached his ears. Even the sound dampeners of the too thick walls and their magic infused layers could muffle it fully.

The drag and thud wasn't shifter or troll. Sentinel.

They'd loosed them in the prison.

Not an unusual occurrence.

Fin. Hear me.

He waited a beat, but got no response. Telepathy wasn't in his wheelhouse of skills either. That was all Fin. If the little fucker listened for him, he would be able to respond. Then again, it might be the prison itself. He was a few levels lower than planned, and escapes usually triggered stronger defenses.

Fin was on his own.

Clever bastard could figure it out.

The shuffling steps continued along the hall, but Maddox held off facing his charge until after the sentinel's steps faded in the distance.

They'd have to sit it out for a few hours at least.

Pivoting, he met the baleful glare of his charge. Instead of saying anything, she merely raised her eyebrows, then held out her wrists. The rich tang of copper hit his nose at the same instant, and saliva flooded his mouth. Concern drenched his earlier rage as the blood ran in rivulets from her savaged wrists.

"Fuck," he swore and reached for the first shackle. Pressure applied in the right spot should release them, but they refused to budge. The metal itself had begun to sink into her wrists.

Lips compressed to a thin white line, she stared at him with fiery retribution in her eyes. The shackle didn't release as he continued to press into it, and the blood slicking her arms began to pool on the floor. The overwhelming fragrance with its sensuous notes of bourbon soaked vanilla stoked a hunger he hadn't experienced in well over five hundred years.

The magic in the shackles wouldn't release. Renewed anger flooded him. So far, this retrieval had turned into a clusterfuck. "You shouldn't have run," he growled at her, and she shifted her fingers, curling three of them and her thumb, leaving only her middle fingers extended at him. "Very cute, Kitten."

"Stop calling me that."

He considered it for a beat before he gave her a smile that was more grimace than grin. "Sorry, Kitten, no can do." He didn't mean the apology about her name but about the fact he had to grip and tear the shackles. The metal screamed and fought him as he wrenched the first one open. The magic zapped along his arms, and the unpleasant odor of singed hair polluted the air.

Fiona didn't make a sound as he ripped the first shackle off. The horror of her flesh would haunt him for a while. Blood dripped steadily, even after he removed it. Fortunately the second one didn't fight him and responded to the correct pressure points, popping open.

"What the fuck are those things?"

Maddox stared at the dwarven-forged cuffs. They'd cost him his weight in gold and had held everything from a mad troll to a wild vampire in a feeding frenzy without ever breaking.

And he'd had to use the fact they were keyed to him to destroy them.

"It doesn't matter," he said, tossing them into the sink to be cleaned. Maybe he could fix the other cuff later. Doubtful, but worth a try. He went to take her hands and lift her bloodied wrists to his lips, but she pulled free.

"Let me help," he ordered, and she rolled her eyes.

"I've had enough of your help. You know, I was having a really lovely day before you showed up with your bitching, snarling, and moaning—not to mention your murder bracelets. I don't mind kink, hot stuff, but I draw the line at fire games."

Fire...

"They weren't fire-infused, but cold forged. They shouldn't have done that." They'd never responded to anything or person he'd shackled before like that. "If you won't let me lick them, Kitten, then you should."

"Why the fuck am I going to lick my bloody and mangled wrists?"

Because they were still bleeding, even if sluggishly, and she had grown paler. The puddle grew wider as well as deeper. Done with the argument—all the arguments—he pounced. Tossing her onto the narrow cot, he dropped down to pin her, even as her eyes blazed. He narrowly caught her forearms before she clawed him with her hooked fingers.

Running his tongue over her ravaged flesh, he damn near moaned aloud. Despite the stench of the other male, her blood tasted sweeter than nectar and twice as potent. Even the lingering hints of magical steel decorating the wounds couldn't detract from its potency.

Hunger ripped through his beast with a kind of ferocity he hadn't experienced since he'd settled into his first true transformation. Man, animal, and vampire lived in harmony, but right now, both vampire and beast fought to lap up every drop. Her musk deepened, grew more refined, and even as the wounds closed on one wrist, he turned to suck gently against the other.

Cock painfully swollen, he ground his hips at hers, and she arched her head back as a low moan vibrated from her throat. Fierce desire fisted him, and he gazed at the slender column of her throat as he cleaned her wrists and hands of every drop and scrap of blood. He sucked on her fingers, and she let out another of those delicious moans that vibrated from her throat like a true purr.

Definitely his kitten. Only when her hands and wrists were clean and the skin shiny and pink from fusing closed, did he push her arms up and shackle her wrists with his hands this time—one hand to be precise. With his free hand, he caught her chin and tilted her face so he could see the color in her lips. Still too pale, but there.

She opened her eyes. The amber color of them drowned out by fat, blown pupils, and her scent grew all the more intoxicating.

"You need to feed." His voice came out too animalistic, rough, and raw. The rumble of his beast stalking through each word.

"No," she husked the word, and he reared his head back. Her languid smile taunted him. "I don't. Trust me, I'm well-sated."

He'd kill the bastard. It wasn't just about territory anymore. Whoever that male was, he'd never live to whisper about having touched her, much less think about it. The only one who would be sating her from now on would be him.

When her purr turned to a laugh, he glared at her. "You might have been sated." He refused to use the word 'well.' "But you're still a newborn. Blood is vital to you, you need to drink plenty and often. The stronger the blood, the less you'll have to feed."

"I'm not a vampire," she informed him. "I'm a succubus. I've always been a succubus. I don't feed on blood."

She hitched her thighs around his hips, and one minute, he blanketed her, and the next, he was on his back on the hard stone floor. His skull rapped against the surface with a blow that stunned him. His kitten straddled him, grinding against his aching cock even as she gave him a vicious smile.

When he would have gripped her hips, she smirked and then stood. His whole body shook with want of her. Not even the other male's stench was a deterrent. More, it served as enticement to remove it and replace it with his own, until he branded her with it.

His beast snarled as she looked down at him, her expression almost disdainful.

"Your lust is a magnificent thing, hot stuff. But as I said earlier, I'm full." Then she casually stepped over him like he wasn't even there. Skirting the pool of blood she paced over to the sink where she lifted the shackles up and out with two fingers and dropped them on the floor like they were a distasteful.

Disbelief rocked through him as she cranked on the water and began to wash her hands. Before he could growl or even summon his language skills, she stripped off her top, giving him an eyeful of her slender back and the fresh bruises littering her flesh.

His mind stuttered to a halt as she raised her damp hands to her wild tumble of red hair and then began to twist it up, tucking it into itself in a knot.

The fact that she shed her pants nearly made him swallow his tongue. What fresh hell was this? With cupped hands, she splashed water over herself, and he tracked every droplet as it skated over her soft flesh.

Until he zeroed in on the very present, deeply imbedded handprints bruising those hips he'd wanted to hold while he fucked into her.

Their presence doused his lust in ice water.

The hot rage turned cold. Every little thing he learned just made him want to kill this asshole more. But now...now he wanted to make him suffer while he died. He'd put his hands on what was not his.

"You should stop growling so much," she commented in that low, sex-drenched voice. "It's very unattractive."

Maddox snorted. He didn't need any of his senses to confirm the mistruth. "Liar."

She glanced over her shoulder as she worked water down her arms, sluicing away any last minute traces of the blood— and his saliva. Still, Maddox sat up and didn't move to interfere.

The show was definitely worth it, and if she managed to rinse herself of that stench, it would be much better for both of them. He didn't need to be battling with his urges to erase it himself, and it would settle his beast. His vampire had given up trying.

Not many understood the clear lines of distinction he experienced with his aspects. It was a delicate balance, one he'd maintained for centuries.

Until today.

The hellion utterly ignoring him as she bathed from the sink captivated him in a way he'd never experienced. Instead of plotting their way out, he debated the different ways he could lure her back over to the bed. Dominating her was definitely one way, but she had too much fight in her to submit to him yet.

Begging wasn't an option.

He would never take without permission, no matter how badly he wanted her. Even aware she'd stripped for the sole purpose of punishing him wouldn't make him breach that inviolable wall.

He murdered men who did that.

No, Maddox had only one choice. He would have to seduce her and earn her trust. Then convince her she wanted to submit to him. That she wanted him to claim her. It would be much sweeter for both of them that way.

He was a hunter, and he'd never failed to get his prey.

They couldn't hide her deep enough in this dungeon turned prison to escape him. He could be patient.

It would have been nice to know before the shackles, though.

His beast settled, and his vampire surged, even as the man took his place at the peak of the pyramid. Once they had the nature of the hunt, nothing stopped them.

"You're smiling," Fiona said, half-turned and revealing the spectacular curve of her breasts. They were crowned with strawberry shaded nipples that made him hungry for summer.

"I'm enjoying the view, Kitten," he told her honestly.

She rolled her eyes and turned away, leaving him with her glorious ass on display and the occasional glimpse of pink lips when she bent over. Yes, he had the taste of this hunt, and while she might think she was denying him, he would lap up every single moment.

Where are you? Fin's voice pinged against him.

It was about damn time. *In Hell with a nymph. Where the fuck are you?*

Where I'm supposed to be. Why haven't you rendezvoused? The guards are everywhere, and they're about to let out the warden's corspesnare.

That could be bad.

Course, it also meant they'd just have to stay in this cell.

Are you safe?

His only response was a mental snort followed by *Do you have her?*

Not quite yet. *Yes.*

We'll adjust the plan.

They were going to have to.

"You're still smiling," Fiona challenged as she faced him a split-second before she pulled her top back on. The color didn't suit her in the least, and yet, she turned the drab fabric into something glorious because it touched her skin.

"We might be here a while," he said as he rose and then sprawled on the cot, stretching out. He'd slept on stone that was more comfortable. Even with his eyelids half-lowered, he didn't miss her stepping into her pants and pulling them up.

No panties.

At all.

He approved.

"So you're just going to nap?"

He patted the cot next to him. "Plenty of room, you can sleep on me if you like."

"Generous," she deadpanned.

"I can be."

Arms folded, she glanced from him to the door. "Some rescue plan."

"Not done yet, Kitten. Now sheathe your claws and come give us a cuddle."

She flipped him off and moved to the far corner where she sat down with her back to the wall and her eyes half-closed.

Eh, it was worth a try.

Maddox? Fin reached out.

Hmm?

Is it true? Hope and anticipation curled in Fin's mental voice.

Was she a hybrid like them?

Yes. He confirmed. *She's ours.*

Fin didn't respond in words, but the enormous satisfaction swelling through the connection made Maddox smile again.

"Keep smiling over there, hot stuff. You're still in a cell."

"I know," he answered. "You're still with me."

"Yay." The single dry syllable enticed him to laugh all over again.

She didn't like him.

But she also didn't know him.

Not yet.

CHAPTER 4

"The first step towards getting somewhere is to decide that you are not going to stay where you are." - Unknown

Twelve or so hours after the male interrupted my mental building, I finally managed to get the house's construction perfect. The bluff it would sit upon was somewhere along the California coast. It would make for spectacular sunsets in the evening over the water. The deck above would allow me to greet the sun in the mornings.

I really missed the sun. Weird to think about the things you lose. No, not because of that idiot vampire, but because I'd landed up here, consigned to the Nightmare Penitentiary for the crime of fucking up someone's idea of what was natural.

Hybrids couldn't possibly exist. On that note, I agreed with them. I wasn't a vampire. I'd died—theoretically—then woke up to whatever these physiological changes were I'd undergone. The transformation left me exhausted, starving, and really, really irritated.

How had Elias described me once?

Oh, right, Psychotic Monster Syndrome.

The humming leftover buzz—what little of it remained from Dorran's visit—had waned. The lightheadedness began with the blood pouring out of my wounded wrists. Before my latest captor decided to get all finger, wrist, and hand licking good with cleaning me up. The fact the wounds closed explained the shivers of awareness rippling through my system, and it had nothing at all to do with the intensity in his eyes as he worked to repair what his nasty little toys had done.

Nothing at all.

The torches had gone out in the corners. If this level were like my own, then night had fallen. The time for Dorran's potential visit approached. Only there would be no visit because I wasn't on my level—probably not even then. It hadn't been a full twenty-four hours since his last call. He rarely came two nights in a row. In the beginning? Yes. Not anymore.

I'd been well fed.

Emphasis on the past tense.

The blood loss also explained the electric need to roll around in the lust roiling off the snarl-monkey currently sprawled on the bed like some over-sized lazy ass cat, expanding to take up all the room.

I eyed him, then the door. He'd done something to it, but I hadn't tested it—yet. Not as long as sentinels shuffled in the hall. It had been a few hours, though. Maybe they'd moved on.

Could be they hadn't noticed my absence. The only person I'd seen since my arrival *was* Dorran. Even the blood bags arrived through a slot in the door.

I sighed.

"Something wrong, Kitten?"

I didn't bother to answer.

My name wasn't fucking *Kitten*.

Back to the house…

"You know," he said, almost idly. "I'm here to help you."

…I wanted something hedonistic in the bathroom. A huge tub, something I could practically swim in, as well as just languish and soak. When was the last time I had a *real* shower much less a bath? One upside to the vamp blood, I supposed, was the lack of body hair growth. This long without a real chance to groom, and I should look like Bigfoot.

I could stand the hair on the legs, not the hair in my pits. Nope. Just made me itch thinking about it.

But the lack of even the appearance of stubble was definitely an upside.

"You are a stubborn little hellion, aren't you?" The amusement curving through the words wasn't remotely sexy. "*Kitten*."

Definitely a big tub, jets, too. I could do bubble baths, or crank it up to something churning.

Oh. A splash guard would be—

From indolent to action, Maddox suddenly loomed over me in my corner, his eyes blazing. When hot fingers cupped my chin and yanked my gaze up to his, I curled my fingers. I did not give him permission to touch me. "You go ahead and claw at me if you need to," he told me in a raspy voice. "You can scowl, you can even kick me in the balls—though I'd prefer not to repeat that experience—what you don't get to do is ignore me."

I snorted. The weight of his thumb along my jaw sent heat curling through my system. It was colder on this level than it had been on mine. Maybe it was just the fact that I'd been sitting against the stone for hours and it had leached all the heat from my body. Not that it mattered. I wasn't in any danger of freezing to death. My eyes had adjusted fine to the near-total darkness the extinguishing torches plummeted us into. But I didn't need the night sight to make him out.

The son of a bitch's eyes glowed.

"You know, Kitten, it's rude to withhold your tongue. Even if all it has to say are scathing things."

"Are you bored?" I asked abruptly, and surprise flickered through his eyes.

"No," he answered after a beat, keeping his hand firm on my jaw.

"Neither am I. Now fuck off."

A growl rumbled in his chest, but I flicked my gaze to the left of his and let my eyes go unfocused. The bathroom could be done in blue tones…

The grip on my jaw tightened and then released abruptly. I kept my gaze trained elsewhere, but the jerk of him scooping me off the floor yanked my attention to the present. "Are you impaired in some way?" I demanded, ignoring the hard chest he cradled me against or the fact that heat from his body licked across mine like a cheerful fire crackling in the fireplace.

His snort seemed to echo mine from earlier, but he didn't answer as he stood and carried me back over to the bed he'd been occupying. When he settled, he didn't lie down so much as sit with his back braced against the wall and me in his lap.

The very hard cock beneath my ass wasn't remotely comfortable. Maybe I should have kicked him harder.

"Get some sleep, Kitten," he rumbled. "If you can."

"Did anyone ask you?" I flattened a hand against his chest to shove away, but it was like being bound in steel. The heat seemed to rise off of him in shimmering waves, chasing away the stone chill buried in my bones.

"No," he murmured, almost agreeably before he nuzzled his face against my hair.

"If you start licking me again, I'm going to tie a knot in your dick so tight, you'll be screaming when you take a piss."

Dead silence greeted my proclamation. Then he began to shake. The soft vibration and huffs of barely suppressed laughter rocked him. Since he had me all wrapped up in the steel bands of his arms and curled against his too hot, too hard body, it rocked me, too.

"Kitten," he said in between growling chuckles. "You're a delight."

Oh, just fucking kill me.

I rolled my eyes and tipped my head back, uncaring if he thought I bared my throat to him. For the record, I wasn't, but what I debated was whether I should slam my head into his face again. I still had a headache from earlier, but it would be worth it to shut him up.

When he dragged his nose along my throat, however, I froze. Every instinct I possessed began to scream. I curled my fingers at the first deep inhale he took, and tried to ignore the way my skin pebbled and my pussy clenched when he exhaled and the warmth of his breath eddied over my flesh.

Liquid warmth spilled through my system, chasing the chill from my veins, and I squirmed to find a more comfortable place to sit than the hard cock jabbing me right in the ass. He pressed his lips right over my pulse point, but at my next wriggle, his teeth grazed the skin and I scowled.

"You bite me, and I will end you."

His laughter huffed against my skin, even as he began to move his mouth along my throat in a half caress, half nibbling motion. His teeth added just the promise of sting, and I wasn't clenching my ass or my pussy in anticipation of that bite.

No, I absolutely wasn't.

"The last son of a bitch who bit me nearly drained me to death," I said in as icy a controlled tone as I could manage given the conflicting messages of 'no' and 'oh fuck yes' my body seemed to be giving out. The musk of his desire scented the air heavily around me, a cloud of choking testosterone and something so very decadently other that I had to fight against sucking it in greedily.

Whatever he was, he smelled divine.

It, I mentally corrected. It. Not he.

A pause, then a soft kiss and the rasp of his stubble against my flesh like he was rubbing his cheek against my throat. Fuck me, that actually felt good.

"What was his name?" The question slid through me, inviting me to answer, beckoning as surely as if he'd slid his fingers into my wet pussy and crooked them until I saw stars.

Stop it.

My traitorous body needed to shitcan those thoughts right now. I was *not* hungry, and contrary to all the lovely rumors about my kind, I didn't just spread my legs for every dick I met.

Not even hard, hot dicks that would probably take some effort to engulf and would likely drill me until I saw stars.

Nope, not doing it.

What was the name of the fucker who drained me to the brink of death then force-fed me his blood? Not happening.

When I caught up to him—and I would—I planned to break his legs and then every other joint in his body, give him just enough blood to heal, then start over.

A few centuries of that, and I might get bored.

Asshole.

"You can tell me, Kitten," Maddox invited in that sexy baritone. "I promise to share, but I'd rather end your maker before he recalls the persuasive power he might have over you."

That made me laugh. "He can't control me."

The idea was so patently ridiculous, I couldn't stop the chuckles shaking me. He lifted his head abruptly as I ran a hand over my face trying to suppress the mirth. The riveted stare suggested he'd never heard a woman laugh before.

How sad for him.

"All vampires can control their get, at least in the beginning. It's how baby vamps are kept from going absolutely mad and slaughtering whole villages." Then he seemed to consider it and shrugged. "Unless, of course, that's what you want to happen. Beyond that, only the most powerful can control another vamp."

"The prince of the city couldn't control me, sugar, trust me. My so-called maker couldn't either. Probably because, wait for it, I'm *not* a vampire."

The gentlest stroke of his fingers eased beneath the hem of my shirt and caressed the flesh there. It was pleasant, not provocative, so I didn't break his hand. "Are you sure about that?"

"Yes." No doubt existed in me on that front at all. "Ugh, why am I talking to you? I have a bathroom to build."

"Perhaps because I'm here," Maddox suggested. "And you're not shivering from the cold anymore."

I hadn't been shivering before.

"It could also be, I'm on your side and came to rescue you."

"Well, you're doing a bang-up job so far," I remarked. "How's that going for you?"

"Challenging," he admitted. "Yet, you won't hear me complaining about the time together."

I rolled my eyes. Not charmed.

"Then what was all that growling and shackling earlier, hmmm?" Yeah, wiggle out of that one.

"The shackles, I apologized for," he said, catching my hand and lifting it to press his lips against my wrist.

"Not that I heard."

"No?" A tease.

"No." I kept my tone flat.

"Hmm." Another kiss placed right over my pulse point that had absolutely nothing to do with the tautness in my core. I wasn't hungry.

Why was I getting all soft and cuddly?

Ugh.

I would not be one of *those* women.

Or even one of those succubi.

"Then please accept my apologies, Kitten," he murmured against my skin, the vibrations sending little shocks racing up my arm. "The intention was never to harm you."

"Huh."

He lifted his head, and his eyes shimmered as he stared at me. Interesting. All pretense of humanity abandoned those slitted eyes.

"What are you?" I asked before I could think better of opening that door.

"Curious, Kitten?"

I jerked my wrist from his clasp and slapped his chest. "Stop. Calling. Me. That."

"No," he answered with too much of a smile in his voice. He cradled me closer as though he wanted to tuck my head against his shoulder. I didn't want to get much closer than I already was. The man's scent seemed everywhere, like a cloud that wanted to hug me.

"Why not?"

"Because you're sharp toothed and clawed, like a kitten," he murmured, then pressed a kiss to my forehead. When I jerked my head back, he didn't seem remotely perturbed by the action. "You're impulsive and headstrong. You're doing things without an ounce of consideration for the fact that you're alone with a much older, much stronger, and far more dangerous being than yourself." His voice dropped an octave as he reached the end of his not-threat.

"Far more dangerous than me?" I almost purred—fuck that analogy, really, but I did it anyway—and narrowed the distance to his face myself this time. I cupped his cheek, the rasp of stubble prickling my palm. His slitted eyes constricted, but the glow behind them intensified. Shifting until his lips were a breath from mine, I met his stare unblinking. His body went taut, and the band of steel around my back tightened further as his fingers dug into my side. "I don't know about that," I whispered. His sharp intake of breath made me smile. "I'll give you old and cranky," I said after a pregnant pause. "But dangerous? Hardly."

The split-second between his pupils' constriction and sudden expansion warned me of his intention, and as soon as he darted his head forward to claim my lips, I wrenched his head sideways.

I didn't snap his neck, but the action promised I could have, and I held his head tight, not releasing my grip even when his own turned bruising.

"Don't presume you know me," I whispered through clenched teeth. "I didn't ask for your help. I didn't ask for you to come here. You don't own me. No one does."

"Fuck, that's hot," a new voice said from behind me, startling the fuck out of me. I scrambled to disentangle myself from resting dick face. Not that I needed to bother, he'd already risen and tossed me behind him on the cot as he lunged to put himself between me and our new arrival.

Instead of an immediate fight, Maddox laughed. "You always did know how to make an entrance."

"Been here a few minutes," the new voice said, though I couldn't make out more than a faint outline of negative space in the dark. "But you two were being all cuddly, I didn't want to step on your moment. Should have known better, brute. Your lack of charm seems to have rubbed our lady the wrong way."

The possessiveness in that last sentence irked. With a light slap, the owner of the voice sidestepped Maddox and then seemed to hover over me. Top notes of ginger, grapefruit, and cardamom teased a clean, almost playful essence, but the vetiver, cedar, and the rich loam of freshly turned earth cautioned me.

"Has Maddox been being his normal, boorish self?" Sympathy and humor weaved through his voice. "He means well, he really does."

"Fuck off, Fin," Maddox growled. "Kitten, this is Fin. Our ticket out. Fin, this is Kitten."

"Kitten?" 'Fin' sounded almost insulted. "Maddox, the lovely lady has a name. Don't you, darling?"

The sweetness in his voice threatened to choke me, or maybe send me to a dentist. Instead of answering, I turned my glare on where Maddox stood. "Why are there now two of you?"

"Ignore her, she's been in here too long," Maddox stated. "Has the breach calmed down?"

"No," Fin said before he dropped to sit next to me on the cot. Only—there was an absolute absence of warmth. If Maddox was the sun, this guy was the cold, dark void. How did he have such a powerful scent and absolutely no heat?

And why couldn't I be left alone to design my house?

"In fact, it's worse," Fin sounded almost cheerful about the fact. "The warden's pacing the levels, going one by one. Did you know he's a shadow demon?"

Maddox growled.

Fin leaned toward me. "Don't mind him, he gets a little grouchy about demons of all kinds. Present company excepted, of course."

"She's not a demon," tall, dark, and growly snarled. He said it with almost the same amount of force I'd used when I told him I wasn't a vampire.

Weird.

"Anyway," Fin said, with a wave of his hand. I couldn't quite make him out, even this close. My night vision was good, even with the absence of light, but it was like he was undefined. "They're really hot to find her. That, or they're just having a dick measuring contest with how much security they can throw out there. The corpsesnare is wandering, Sentinals are out, there's like three times the number of normal guards at all the exits, and I almost ran into Brina."

He gave an indelicate shudder on the last.

"We should be fine here for a couple of days," Maddox said, and despite the definitiveness of the statement, his tone didn't suggest the same.

"Maybe," Fin said. "Maybe not. I sent for Rogue."

"Why the fuck did you do that?" Oh, that pissed him off. His anger flooded the room with so much delicious heat, I sighed and stretched. I swore his eyes glowed even brighter, enough to give more definition to the room, but not to Fin.

"He sounds really pissy, but he's just frustrated," Fin told me, head tilted toward me as if confiding state secrets. "Rogue's not a people person anymore, but he's also more than capable of creating the distraction we need to get out of here." The last he directed at Maddox. "So just simmer down and cool the fire breathing."

Fire breathing?

A growl resonated through the room. "Fin, Rogue won't just cause a *distraction*. We haven't summoned him in over a century."

"So?"

"So, do you recall the *last* time we had to call him?"

"Yeah but that was totally different," Fin countered. "One, we had no way of knowing what those trolls were hiding, and two, if the scouts hadn't shot first and tried to ask questions later, he wouldn't have slaughtered them."

I had to admit, I was getting more curious by the minute.

"And to be totally fair," Fin continued. "We were this close to getting our heads chopped off."

"That's because *someone* doesn't know how to follow a plan." That someone was clearly Fin. I'd just met him, and the fact he had impulse issues couldn't be clearer if he'd taken out a neon advertising sign.

"Oh, I know how to follow a plan," Fin argued in a smooth tone, then leaned toward me. "I definitely know how to follow a plan, it's just that when it's a stupid plan, I like to get creative."

His shoulder brushed mine, and the sense of nothingness hit me. My palms itched to reach out and put a hand on him.

"Fin," Maddox growled. "When did you send for Rogue?"

"About an hour before we left." The cheerfulness in his voice pulled a reluctant smile from me. The fact Maddox actually exhaled the most put upon sigh so heavily made me laugh.

The chuckle worked its way up from my belly, and I shook from it. I *almost* felt sorry for Maddox.

Almost.

But really, fucking with his day? Couldn't happen to a nicer guy.

"She thinks I'm funny," Fin said with a grin in his voice. "You like me best, don't you?"

Still chuckling, I almost answered in the affirmative, in spite of the fact that I would rather be back on my rather monotonous routine if I had to be stuck in this place. Probably better to *not* encourage them. Then again, Maddox's derisive snort made me rethink that. Dropping my hand onto Fin's thigh, I said, "I absolutely do like you better."

Not best.

But better.

There, suck on that dick face.

I didn't really get to savor Maddox's response though, because that sense of nothingness regarding Fin only intensified. No heat. No pulse. No sense of him being *there*, and yet, I could touch him.

"You're astral projecting." Shock rippled through me.

"Very good, beautiful," Fin complimented me. "I was supposed to meet you hours ago, but apparently, Maddox doesn't know his ups from his downs and totally screwed the pooch on the introductions. I didn't want to wait a couple more days, so—voila. Here I am, and not too soon, if you don't mind me bragging."

Another aggrieved sigh from Maddox made me smile wider. Fin could really push his buttons.

Still...

"To be fair, he could have been out of here, but he insisted on following me." I shrugged. "I'm the one who came down the stairs instead of up. Oops."

"It's all right, anyone could get turned around in here. Sometimes down is the way to go. Who knows, by the time Rogue gets here, you might have to go down to get up, and then we'll go right to get left. It'll be a whole thing. But we'll both be here to help Maddox out so he doesn't get lost."

"You really aren't helping," Maddox said, his tone bland and bored before he moved back to the cot. When he dropped to sit right on top of Fin, I expected more of a protest than an exasperated sigh.

Then the shadow disconnected itself from him and stood. "You know I hate it when you do that."

"Amazing the things we do that we know will irritate the other."

"True," Fin admitted. "I'm guilty of that." Then he turned to me again, and the shadowy hand came to rest against my thigh this time as he knelt. "I'm honored to meet you, Fiona MacRieve, I don't know if I said that earlier."

"No," I told him. "Not really. But I'll bite, why are you honored?"

"You're the—"

"Fin." Maddox's snarl cut him off. "Later. For now, find us a route out of here preferably *before* Rogue arrives. This is an extraction, not a war."

"Eh," Fin, said. "It's kind of both. Even you have to admit that. With the lovely Fiona here the prize at the center of the maze. We just have to get through all the mini-bosses to the big boss, and boom, we get the girl."

"Okay," I said, removing his shadowy hand off my thigh with two fingers. "Bored now."

"Ha." You could practically taste the smirk in Maddox' tone.

"First, no one asked for rescue. Second, I'm not some helpless damsel. Third, I'm nobody's fucking prize."

"I can't wait to lay my real eyes on you when we rescue you," Fin said. "You're *delightful*."

Then he vanished, and it took everything I had not to scream.

"Do either of you actually listen?" I demanded.

Maddox shrugged before he looped an arm around my shoulders and dragged me against the furnace of his body. If I really were a kitten, I'd sink in my claws and shred him before I sprawled out to doze in the heat. I'd almost forgotten what it was like to be surrounded by this much warmth. The only heat I'd had came when Dorran...

"Oh." Fin popped back in and gave Maddox a start. His

jerk betrayed his surprise, which I'd bet on my best pair of shoes—well, second best at any rate, since my best ones got trashed in the same incident that landed me here. "Don't believe a word Maddox says about me. He really does love me, he just doesn't know how to show emotions. He's very sixteenth century in his affections."

Then Fin vanished again, and I chuckled.

"You really do like him," Maddox stated, and I couldn't tell if he was disgusted or pleased by that revelation.

"Don't be jealous," I advised. "I haven't really *met him* met him yet."

"True." That seemed to please him way too much though.

"Then again, I like him more than you—so that's something."

A rumbling growl was his only answer, and I tipped my head to rest against his shoulder and went back to designing my house. Better to not get attached to anything. 'Cause the first opportunity I had, hasta la vista, grumpstiltskin, and his nutty buddy, Fin.

CHAPTER 5

"Reality doesn't impress me. I only believe in intoxication, in ecstasy, and when ordinary life shackles me, I escape, one way or another. No more walls." - Anais Nin

The sudden tension cording the arm I dozed against as the torches whooshed to life in the corners of the room woke me. "It's morning," I told him, then let my eyes fall closed again. The heat rolling off him probably shimmered the air, but I wasn't going to complain.

"That's the only marker for time shifts?" Dislike crackled between the words.

"Well, I ordered the turn down service and breakfast in bed, but the service here is you get what you get and you don't throw a fit." A yawn elongated the last word.

When he rumbled a growl, I leaned away and began to stretch. Fine, if he was awake, it was hard to justify using him as a pillow. Though to be fair, I didn't think he'd actually slept. It was more like he'd just been quiet, and I could sleep without remorse for using him as a pillow.

The arm he had around me tightened, and he dragged me back with a huff. "You don't have to move," he said, then pressed his chin to the top of my head. He was a big dude, but I wasn't a damn doll.

"If you're talking, you're up," I told him, and peeled his hand away from my waist as I stood. The room swayed, but I locked my legs to keep from falling on my ass. The last thing I wanted was to give Mad Dog Twenty there a chance to scoop me up.

As soon as I was sure I wouldn't collapse, I made my way to the toilet in the corner. Dropping my drawers, I took a seat and emptied my bladder. Some people would be put off by being on display. Me? Not so much. I didn't invite him. He was just lucky I didn't have to crap. I had no problems with giving him a stink bomb he would remember.

Finishing, I flushed the evidence then stripped out of the top and pants to begin my daily wipe down. The water from the sink was always cold. But it was clean, and there was no taint to it. The ache in my wrists served as the only reminder of the damage the shackles had done. He'd done a very effective job cleaning the injuries. Had he healed them or just sealed the injuries? I'd certainly burned enough resources in the recovery, so it was a fifty-fifty debate on who owed what to whom.

The items in question were no longer on the floor. He must have recovered them when his friend beamed in for a visit. Ignoring the chill, I wiped down the best I could with what passed for soap. What I wouldn't give to wash my hair in a real shower. So far, I'd made do with washing it in the sink, but there was no conditioner, and even my hair needed something. Dipping my head, I twisted to get it under the water.

A pained groan issued from behind me, and I rolled my eyes.

"Don't look if you can't handle it," I told him.

"Oh, I can handle you just fine," Maddox informed me. "Though you're lucky it's me and not someone else. Not everyone would be so restrained."

I snorted. "No one takes anything from me," I reminded him as I worked the soap through my hair. Eyes closed, I massaged my scalp. "And intentions matter."

"Fair." The single grunt was his only response. I appreciated his lack of challenging the assertion. All things being equal, I didn't need to deal with another flood of choking testosterone. That said, I didn't question the fact he wouldn't try to take what hadn't been offered to him.

Like I said, intentions mattered. His lust hung over him like a cloud of electricity, buzzing the air with its presence. But he also hadn't moved from his spot on the cot, nor had his focus lasered on to me. After rinsing the soap out, I wrung the hair as best I could, then straightened.

I almost objected to putting the clothes back on, but I didn't have anything else to wear, so clean or dirty, the ugly drab gray would have to do. The top clung to me in places, and my dripping hair soaked the back. The chill raced over my flesh, but I ignored it as I stepped into the pants.

Unsurprisingly there were no blood bags on the floor. That was a nice change of pace. I never touched the damn things anyway. Finished, I headed for the corner I'd sat in the day before when Maddox released a warning growl and stood. The cell suddenly seemed far too small for the two of us as his presence billowed out, carrying heat with it that chased away my chill.

"Sit."

"Not a dog."

The baleful look he sent me promised a hell of a fight,

then he exhaled. "Kitten...*don't* provoke me. This whole situation is grating on my nerves. I do not want to take it out on you."

The request surprised me. It wasn't an order. The fact that he asked followed by the explanation pleased me on a level I wasn't going to examine at the moment. Instead, I had a counter offer. "Answer a question for me?"

If my response surprised him, he gave no indication. In the light from the torches, he seemed even bigger than he had the day before. His shadow stretched even further across the walls, even as his eyes reflected the flickering flames. They weren't slitted at the moment, but more normal. The hazel-green a pretty enough color. Almost simple.

Yet nothing about Maddox was at it appeared.

That much I didn't doubt.

He shrugged. "Ask."

"Why are you here? I mean really. Why come to get me? You don't know me. We've never met before." I'd have remembered him. "So why risk it to get in here?" This place was legend. Most who were consigned within its walls never returned. Those rare few who had? Well, it was said they weren't the same.

Granted, rumors and urban legends weren't precisely facts, but they were all I had to work with.

"Because what you are isn't a crime," he said simply. "And we take care of our own."

While vastly unspecific, it was an answer. Before I could press the point, a shuffle and scrape from the hallway seemed to echo in the silence. We both stilled, but Maddox went from looming over the bed to next to the door in the blink of an eye.

That shit was unnerving.

If he could move that fast, how had I outrun him?

Oh. I nailed him in the balls.

Right.

Even supergrunt there needed time to catch his breath.

Good to know.

"We'll get you out of here, Kitten," he continued when I said nothing. "You may trust that if you trust nothing else."

I trusted very little, but sure, why not? Shrugging, I moved back to the bed and took a seat. Crossing my legs, I leaned back against the wall and let my eyes drop half-closed. I was far more tired than I wanted to tell him. The lost blood volume wasn't a problem. Maybe if I hadn't fed so well before, but I was still weary.

Even though I wasn't looking at him, the weight of his stare settled on me like a tangible presence. Finally, he moved to the sink, and from beneath my lashes, I caught the flash of golden skin as he shed his shirt and then washed his face and chest.

The ripple of muscle didn't surprise me. Having been gripped to that steely body, I wouldn't expect anything else. When he finished, he ducked his head under the water, and slicked back his sandy brown hair away from his face. It just gave him a more angular look, not that it was a bad look.

When he turned to use the toilet, I closed my eyes and let him have his privacy.

See, I had manners, unlike some people.

The image of my house flickered to life, and I began to do some rearranging in the room I'd make my bedroom. I wanted it to be as spacious as possible, no walls to hem me in. Having floor to ceiling windows all along one side would help.

Unless the sun turns you into a pile of ashes, then you better invest in a good vacuum for the next residents.

Shoving that wordy bitch out of my head, I debated the color scheme. I wanted blues in the bathroom. The sea and the seashore were good themes. But the bedroom? Soft creams, maybe, nothing too bold. I wanted it to be restful.

Heat settled next to me, and an arm slid around me. I didn't fight the tug as he settled me right against him. I'd actually gotten chilled after the cold wash and the fact that my hair was still wet.

"What are you thinking about so hard you have a tiny frown right here?" He traced a finger between my eyebrows, and I flicked my eyes open to find him studying me intensely. His shirt was back in place, and his damp hair had already begun to dry. Guess all that heat he put off took care of that quick.

The words 'none of your business' lingered on my tongue. Not that what I was doing was really a state secret. "I'm building a house."

Surprise reflected in his narrowed eyes. "A house?"

I nodded. "A retreat. Some place just for me. I'm building it from the ground up, so it's exactly what I want and where I want it."

Closing my eyes, I went back to my room and studied it from floors to ceiling. Carpets, definitely. I might do wood floors or tile in the main body of the house, but I wanted the good carpet in here. Did I want a fireplace?

Yes. Images of a stone fireplace flickered to life, then river rock, I kept shifting the construction.

"Can you show me?"

The voice intruded, and I slid him a look. "What?"

"Show me your house."

"No. I'm not done with it yet."

Despite his seeming repose, nothing about Maddox was relaxed. Likely, he tracked any sound in the hall, though there had been none since the earlier shuffle step. In theory, no one was supposed to be in this cell. We could languish here without detection unless they happened to open it up for a new occupant.

Well, then we were fucked.

"Tell me about it then." The soft invitation in his voice came at a direct contrast to his aggravating and entitled tone of the day before.

"No."

"Well that's rude," he chided me. "We're alone. We have time. You could get to know me."

"Or you could shut up and let me build my house. I've been working on it for weeks. By the time I get out of here, I'll be ready to build it."

To my absolute surprise, he went quiet. I half-waited for him to interrupt again. My focus divided between the half-formed nebulous bedroom and the very much present male currently binding me to his side. When his silence continued, I settled into the work of carpet selection, fireplace construction, and where the bed would go. The room would be open, not cluttered. There would clothing storage in the enormous walk-in. Plenty of space for my clothes and shoes without taking up the bedroom. I wanted nothing to obstruct the walls.

Maybe one of them could be painted with a scene. A mountain glen came to mind—trees, grass, and a crystal lake. It was absolutely stunning and pristine in how untouched it was. I could escape all of humanity there. The peace twisted into my veins, and the lust for it flooded me.

The water was cool, even on the warmest days of summer. The woods and the surrounding mountains boasted plenty of game. The location, tucked away so high, wasn't near any crossroads or passes. To ascend to it would require master climbers and a sure knowledge of the way.

It was the perfect escape from everything and everyone. The longer I stood there, the more I realized it was a very real place. This was no simple painting. I drew back from it until I stood only in my room again, and the wall stretched before me beckoned like a gateway.

Almost as if it were saying, *You know you want to come through. Come, play with me.*

Snapping my eyes open, I glared at Maddox. He was absolutely still next to me, his eyes closed and his breathing deep and regular.

He wasn't asleep though.

"Afraid, Kitten?"

"How are you doing that?"

"He's not," Fin announced in a cheerful voice. "That would be me."

Of course it was.

"Fin," Maddox growled. "Have they reduced their security?"

"Nope," Fin stated. Even in the torchlight, I couldn't quite make him out. The blurring seemed to take him just out of focus. Understanding that he wasn't truly present helped, but it was equal parts irritating to focus on him and intriguing to discover how he pulled it off. "They've increased it."

Maddox let out a growl.

"What was that? 'Oh, thank you, Fin. You're right, Rogue was the perfect one to summon for this situation,'" he mimed the answer to himself, pitching his voice almost perfectly into Maddox's deep rumble. "No problem, Mad. You know, I've only got our best interests at heart." He waved off the make believe gratitude with the air of a cocky grin. "'You're too humble, Fin, it doesn't suit you. You were right, and I was, and yes, I know you don't hear this often, but you should. I was wrong.' Hey, it takes a big man to admit something like that, my friend. Have no worries, I won't lord it over you, much."

A snicker escaped as Maddox snorted. "Keep patting yourself on the back."

"Someone has to," Fin said easily, and I could have sworn he winked at me. "Hang on a little bit longer for us, beautiful Fiona. Rogue will be here at nightfall, then you two move and I'll meet you. Between us, we'll get you out."

"You sound very confident," I told him.

"That would be because Rogue knows what they're hiding here, he won't let them say no. While he's making a lot noise, we'll slip out unnoticed. It's a whole thing. Just trust me."

"She doesn't trust easily," Maddox warned, not that I needed him to answer for me.

"But we've already got a connection, Fi and me," Fin argued. "You just sit over there and be all grumpy in your grumpiness, and let me handle this."

Granted, he was kind of cute and amusing, but Maddox wasn't so bad when he wasn't talking. He definitely made the air warmer.

See, I was using my positive people skills. They did actually exist.

A yawn split my jaw before I could say anything though, and both went a little quiet.

"You feeling okay, Kitten?" Maddox pressed his nose to my hair and took a deep breath.

"She looks a little pale, course, you both do. Firelight's not exactly ideal lighting for determining coloring..." Fin drifted closer. I hadn't really paid attention to his movement the night before. Course, it had also been dark. He didn't quite touch the floor as he moved.

How much effort did it take to do that? Not to mention, what was he that he could do it at all? Astral projection was a rare talent, and most who possessed it didn't advertise it. They made the best spies and, under certain circumstances, excellent assassins.

"She lost a lot of blood yesterday." He motioned to the dark stain on the stone. Yeah, I wasn't going to comment on the fact the stone had all but absorbed all that blood. The dark brownish stain was all that remained of my pooled blood.

"Then feed her, asshole," Fin said abruptly, all trace of playfulness gone from his tone. "You can certainly spare a pint."

"I'm not hungry," I said before Maddox could snarl. The fact that the arm he had around me tensed and the rest of him seemed to vibrate suggested his rather vehement response to the accusation.

Fin jerked his gaze to me.

"And I don't heal that way anyway."

Head tilted, he stared at me. "You do realize you're part vampire, right?"

"You do realize that's an oxymoron, right?" What was it with people telling me what I was? "There's no such thing as a part-vampire." Hybrids didn't exist. Do join the party line. Why else was I in this prison? Oh yeah, because I'd broken some covenant by existing.

Right.

"Agitation. Pallor. Exhaustion. Dissociation, bloodlust, and madness follow. Baby vamps have to eat." He ticked each item off like I was five.

Yeah, my estimation of Fin began to drop by several points. "I'm a succubus," I reminded him. "That's not how I heal." Or feed.

"Well, I'm pretty sure Maddox still remembers how that works, just let him…"

"Fin," Maddox snapped. "She already told you she wasn't hungry. Leave her alone."

Oh ho, he was defending me now? The flip-flop was enough to make anyone a little dizzy.

"Yeah, but she's going to need her strength, and if she's waning after only a day in your company, what's she going to be like tonight?" He folded his arms, and I swore I could almost hear the tapping of his foot, even if it wasn't audible.

"We'll be fine," Maddox stated smoothly. "Speaking of conserving energy, you should."

"Says the one who gets to spend time with her while I lay here under the stone floor with a mouse for company," Fin grumbled.

"Stop bitching and go away," Maddox said in an aggrieved tone. "We'll head up when the torches go out."

"Fine. But she sleeps with me tomorrow." He blew me a kiss before focusing on Maddox again. "You got two days. Fair is fair." Then he was gone before my companion could respond.

"Still like him better, Kitten?"

"Not so much."

He chuckled, then slid his hand up to massage my nape. "He's not wrong. You do need some fresh blood. Feeding your dual nature needs to be something you get used to."

"If that's your polite way of saying 'bite me,' no thank you." I really didn't want blood. The image of Dorran cutting himself so the blood trickled out flashed through my mind, accompanying the hot flavor of it on my tongue.

I shuddered and curled my toes as I closed my eyes. I did not want to want it. I wasn't a vampire.

"The hardest part of the transition is accepting your needs have also transitioned," Maddox said, drawing circles against my shoulder with his thumb. "You have to feed both."

"Or what?" I asked, in spite of my intentions of focusing on my house.

"Or bloodlust will set in. The need to sate yourself on whatever you can get your hands on, and you won't mind killing to get what you need."

I didn't mind killing so much now.

"And you won't be able to tell friend from foe."

That part bugged me a little.

"For those who truly deny themselves, they may lose the thread of who they are entirely. Minds have broken in transition before, it is why those who are turned are carefully curated." He was almost likeable as he handled this conversationally, without his domineering and orders.

"Too bad I missed that memo," I told him, though maybe that was another reason Dorran had taken such an interest in me, particularly when I wouldn't feed. It could also be he just wanted to have a good time. Though it was something to consider on both fronts.

"I'll give you some latitude, Kitten, if I hadn't put the shackles on you—you wouldn't be half-starved now." Before I could deny it, he gave my shoulder a squeeze. "Deny you're hungry all you want, but your body betrays you. You can't stay warm, can you? It's why you're letting me hold you."

I would have wrenched away, but he had an iron grip on me. I debated and discarded a half-dozen responses, then settled for just ignoring him.

"Fine, don't answer. But I know the truth, and deep down, so do you. I will not force you, but if it comes down to a choice between risking your sanity or your fury...well, I'll take your rage, and you will feed. Fin was right, I can more than spare the blood, and it's old enough that it will sate you."

"Confident, aren't you?"

He chuckled. "Very."

"Hmm. Are you done?"

"For the moment."

Nodding, I closed my eyes and returned to my house building. I must have drifted off again because he woke me with a gentle shake, and I snapped my eyes open to find myself not just leaning against him, but curled up in his lap like a slutty cat absorbing all that heat.

Okay, I never said I wasn't a slutty cat.

"Is it time?" I asked, and my voice came out a croak. The torches were out, but as with the night before, his eyes glowed.

"Nearly. Fin said five minutes and we move."

Extracting myself from his lap, I nodded. He set me on my feet, bracing me as my head swam. Yeah. That wasn't a good sign. Fuck, I did not want to drink his blood. Once I was out of here, I'd ditch them and go find some cheerful fucker and seduce him. Then I'd find that asshole vampire and rip his spleen out.

Maybe the so-called prince, too.

I was an equal opportunity bitch slapper.

Maddox said nothing as I made my way over to the sink. I splashed a little water on my face to chase away the sleep. I'd slept a good portion of the day. Then I drank down a couple of palmfuls to wet my throat.

"When we get out there," Maddox said. "You'll stick close to me."

Ah, there he was, the autocratic jerk who issued orders. I'd started to worry he'd been replaced by a kinder, gentler Maddox. No one would want that.

"You will do it," he continued. "Don't make me have to drag you out of here kicking and screaming."

I chuckled. "I already kicked, and you have to be really good to make me scream."

The abrupt silence made me smile wider. Never play the game with me. Turning from the sink, I stared across the void toward the glowing eyes regarding me from their narrow slits.

"Kitten, are you going to cooperate?"

That question was pregnant with all kinds of possibilities.

Then again, so was my answer.

"What's in it for me?"

"Your ticket out of here," he promised. "And a long conversation, a real one, with communication on both sides. After that, you're free to go wherever you like."

Sounded too good to be true.

Probably was just a lure to get me to agree. Once we were out, he could focus on containing me. He also had allies waiting for him, the irascible Fin and the mysterious Rogue.

Not that I couldn't handle multiple men, the more the merrier actually. Still...

"Neutral location for the conversation," I said. "No secret fortress with security in place for my 'protection.'"

"Done."

"And if I say no," I continued crossing toward him slowly. "I'll mean 'no.'"

"Understood. But you'll listen to all of it," he countered. "Not just the opening lines before you cut me off to go build your house."

I could live with that.

"Then you have a deal." I held out my hand. One conversation, and I was free? Yeah, I'd take that deal.

His rough palm glided against mine as he closed his fingers over mine. "Stay with me." With a gentle tug, he pulled me to him then set my hand to his belt. "Grip back here, stay there. No matter what happens, do not get in front of me."

"Even if someone is going to try and skewer you from behind?" I mean really, if he wanted to set explicit terms. "Because if they have to stab me to get to you, I'm probably going to move."

Silence. "Fine. You may take out anyone who comes at us from behind."

"Lover here, RDF, not fighter."

"Now that," he said slowly, his face suddenly close to mine. "Is the first true lie you've told me. I have faith in those claws, Kitten."

A beat.

"It's time. Save all debates, discussions, and arguments for once we're out. Just remember, we have a deal."

"Sir," I purred. "Yes, sir."

He shuddered, and I smiled. When everything has been taken from you and all you have left was revenge, there wasn't much you wouldn't do.

Even take jabs at the so-called rescuer who inserted himself into your problems.

The door clanged open, and we were moving. The hall had more light, which helped.

It also had a very large, very angry looking corpsesnare, who whirled at our presence and stared right at *me*, salivating.

"Maddox?" I said lightly when he stared the other way.

"Just stay with me."

"Yes, well, I just wanted to point out that we might have a problem."

Turning his head, he paused.

The corpsesnare's jaw was open, showing his row of shiny teeth and letting bits of saliva fall to the stone below.

"Hi, Puppy," I greeted him. "Who's a good dog?"

It snarled.

"Kitten?"

"Hmm?"

"What are you doing?"

"Saying hi to the puppy."

"*That* is not a puppy."

Yeah well, I wasn't a kitten either. But we did what we did with what we had. The corpsesnare began to approach, a low growl rumbling from him like an avalanche of rocks tumbling down the mountainside.

I could seduce a lot of things, but I'd never tried it against something so...impressively oversized and radiating barely suppressed rage.

Maddox turned abruptly. "Stay behind me."

No problem. If it ate him, I'd use that as a distraction. Maddox gave me heartburn, and I hadn't even had a bite.

Bracing himself, Maddox seemed to flicker as the corpsesnare continued to approach, his pace deliberate and measured, hackles up and a constant growl rising in volume.

When he was nearly in snapping range, he roared.

Ugh.

Someone needed to give him a breath mint.

CHAPTER 6

"It simply isn't an adventure worth telling if there aren't dragons."
- J.R.R. Tolkien

The corpsesnare's roar redoubled along the hallway and set most of the hair on my body standing on end, including the wild tangle of curls falling from my head. While I would have loved a blow dryer earlier, this was not what I had in mind. Not even close.

For his part, Maddox hadn't moved, not so much as rocked in the face of fetid breath, razor sharp teeth, and a salivating tongue. Even with my hand on his belt, Maddox didn't seem solid, and yet, his presence swelled. The corpsesnare roared again, but he didn't charge.

That was good.

The only lust he displayed at the moment was bloodlust, and it rolled off of him in stomach-curdling waves along with his rotten breath. All at once, Maddox shifted and the air grew hotter, heavier, and...holy shit.

Yeah, I blew that hold onto his belt promise, dropping it like a hot potato as I backed off from the dragon pushing at the walls around us. The stone began to shred as his wings extended. His size was massive, however, far more than the corpsesnare.

Puppy went for another growl, then retreated a step. He didn't give up much ground, snarling and snapping with each motion of withdrawal he took.

Me? I didn't hesitate, I was almost to the stairwell when the corpsesnare lunged and fire flooded the hallway.

I winced at the yelping shriek from the oversized beast. Hands pressed firmly over my ears, I dropped when fire flared down the hallway, and the smell of singed hair burned my nostrils. Oh. That was nasty.

The roar vibrating me to my bones wasn't coming from the corpsesnare. I almost felt sorry for the oversized beasty, particularly when he yelped and pounded away in the opposite direction. All he'd wanted to do was chow down on some prisoner escapees, not his fault one of them turned out to be a damn dragon.

Seriously? Maddox's arrival had turned my day upside down, too. So I got it.

The dragon in the hallway—yes, that sentence actually passed through my head—twisted around, eyes glaring to find me.

Amidst the smoke and haze of debris, I really didn't have time to consider the color of his scales. But those slitted eyes glowing me? I'd know them anywhere. He opened his mouth, displaying an impressive array of teeth. Here was hoping we weren't going to test his morning breath, because how about no?

Still twisting, he knocked more bricks loose, and a metal door screamed as his tail lashed against it, knocking it open.

The explosion of magic lit the hallway up like a Fourth of July bonfire gone wrong.

I had to be honest here, something ran out of that cell he'd just carelessly torn open with his *tail* as it lashed about. His maneuvering that bulk through a hallway nowhere near big enough for him to spread out, not to mention his wings, kicked up more debris. But that thing or person or whatever that ran out of that room?

It made it three steps in my direction when hot stuff there gave me an up-close look at hungry, hungry dragon. The chomp followed by the crunch of bones was both awesome in its display of power and utterly disgusting.

No sooner had he done it and *swallowed* did he look at me. Lowering my hands, I met that stare. "One, if you belch right now, you will find a dick shaped hole where your cock used to be. You might be big and scaly at the moment, but you gotta play shrinky dinky sooner or later." Head cocked, the dragon stared at me, his inner eyelids blinked once. "Second, you better gargle with like industrial strength bleach before you try to bring your mouth anywhere near me."

Just. Saying.

Ugh.

I had never been so utterly turned on and repulsed by the same action.

What? I was complicated. Suck it.

For the most part, Mad-Dragon—that name was totally sticking—huffed a sound that might have been laughter, even as a hint of fire burst from his nose. Was that the dragon equivalent of a giggle-snort? He continued toward me, showering more debris down from above, and his eyes shifted impercep-tibly. The air around him shimmered like a desert mirage.

The temperature in the hallway left me sweating, but I could live with it. Deodorant would have been nice. But who was going to complain? Right, Mad-Dragon of flaming breath and questionable eating habits—I wasn't going to worry about that. He began to draw back to his original size. The flicker of surprise on his face had me twisting and whirling just as a boot scraped the stone not far from me.

Guard uniforms.

I didn't wait for whoever this was to identify themselves, I struck. Fortunately for me—yes, I said I was weird—they were also mid-strike as they swung the equivalent of a glowing billy club in my direction.

Catching his wrist as he was mid-downswing, I twisted and lunged forward, slamming the heel of my hand right at his crotch. Armor or not, the impact sent a jolt up my arm, but he still hissed, and his grip on the billy club of doom faltered. I didn't wait for it to fall as I slid right into him. The lust wafting from him was also tinged with fear. He didn't want me so much as he wanted desperately to contain me.

Too.

Fucking.

Bad.

As the billy club hit the floor, I clasped his face and yanked it down for a kiss. Shock turned him rigid as I soaked in even his watered down lust. It wasn't much, more like the soggy French fry at the bottom of the bag. It filled the hole, but lacked any kind of satisfaction. The guy sagged, and no sooner had I begun to feed, then he was yanked away. I hissed, but Maddox glared at me as he snapped the guy's neck. The man dropped without another word.

"You want to feed, you feed on me. Until then, we're moving."

Well. Fuck you, too.

"Jealousy doesn't look good on you, Dragon Boy M," I told him, but when he snagged me close to him, two things hit me in the same breath.

If I'd thought he was warm in the cell, he was a thousand times hotter in the hall. His skin should be steaming, he was so hot. The second thing? He was naked. Absolutely, gloriously, one hundred percent naked. He was definitely sexy with a capital damn.

The weight of his cock poked at the too thin fabric of my so-called uniform, and I had to tilt my head to meet his gaze. Yeah, there might have been the vaguest amount of drool involved.

Vaguest.

Possibly.

A few drops.

Fuck. Me.

Why did he have to do this now when we were leaving the enforced isolation with the very tiny bed?

As if reading my mind—or maybe my body, 'cause it got there several seconds before my brain did—Maddox dipped his head. Laser focused on that sensuous mouth, it took me a whole extra-half a heartbeat to put my hand over it before he got too close.

He just ate someone or something.

Right.

Big crunch.

Gross. Hot.

"Gargle. With. Bleach." At the reminder, his eyes crinkled and his smirk pressed against my palm. Catching my hand, he bit down on my palm. Not enough to break skin, but enough that the pressure of his teeth sent an answering pulse straight to my pussy.

Really not the time.

Course, now I was hungry, and he'd killed off my limp noodle of a snack. Maybe I'd make him make it up to me later.

No limp noodle here.

No sirree.

After he released my hand, he retrieved a bag I hadn't even noticed him carrying. He had to bend for it, and let me just add, the view going was almost as good as the view of him returning.

Almost.

He dragged a dark shirt on and then pulled on some pants.

Pity.

His boots were gone, as was his belt. Didn't do a damn thing to turn me off, though. Honestly. He looked even better all disheveled, hair askew and shirt hanging open. He slung the bag over his shoulder, and it lay crosswise over his torso.

Yeah, how had I not noticed that?

"Coming?" He gave me an expectant look, and it was my turn to smirk.

"Until I was so rudely blocked?" I let that suggestion hang out there for a minute before I slapped his chest on my way past. "Not even."

His rough chuckle chased after me as we moved in tandem toward the door. "Grip the strap," he ordered before pushing the metal door outward. It gave him some minor resistance, but the door buckled under the force he exerted.

Yep, that just set all kinds of things fluttering. Though brute strength wasn't a turn on by itself. Fuck, I was hungry.

Once in the hall though, all thoughts of eating took a sharp right turn. A dozen guards swarmed toward us.

"Stay with me," Maddox snarled as he waded in.

Yeah. Sure. No problem.

He moved hella fast, and the first jerk forward nearly pulled my arm out of the socket. Yeah, that wasn't working for me. The first guard who tried to drag me away, however, ate my elbow in his teeth. They were mostly shifters. Not that it slowed Maddox down. I was pretty sure these were wolves. They had that eau de wet dog going on for them.

It was all fun and games until one of the bastards bit me. To be honest, when asked about it later, I had no idea what I did so much as I whirled. Letting go of Maddox, I landed on the bastard, all teeth and claws. The first drag of hot blood on my tongue, and I latched. I consumed every drop, the lust for blood he'd been simmering in along with the blood in his veins.

When this prey was ripped away from me, I whirled, intent on clawing out eyes, only to come face to face with a pair of nearly pitch-black eyes with the barest ring of gray around them, dark hair, and a face like an angel.

"Bad for the digestion, Beautiful."

Oh, I knew that voice.

"That's it. Focus on me."

I was focused on him.

"You about done there, Maddox? This is a lot of fighting for the sweet baby."

Then Maddox was there, he had a hold of my arm and turned me slightly. "Fucker tore right through her shoulder."

Oh. Yeah. Someone bit me. I turned to go after said fucker, when Fin caught my free arm.

"Nope, he's very dead, Beautiful. I promise. Time to go though." Everything but the two of them seemed to be coming from a great distance.

"You're overdoing it," Maddox snarled.

"I can't help it if she's more naturally drawn to me," Fin said smoothly, giving me a charming smile. My heart gave a distinct double-thump. He really was gorgeous, and his voice was buttery soft. I gave into the impulse to lean toward him, but Maddox's grip on my arm kept me from going too far.

Pain lit up along my shoulder and raced across my skin.

"None of that," Fin murmured, pressing a kiss to my wrist. "Nothing hurts. We're going to get out of here, okay?"

I exhaled a long breath. "Okay." That really did sound like a great idea.

"Let's go, straight up," Fin ordered. "Ten levels." He swept me up into his arms, and it made Maddox release me. The poor Mad-Dragon let out a very disgruntled sound. "You first, we need to move fast. I doubt she can keep up with either of us, so let's go."

The world blurred past. The throb in my shoulder returned, and bit-by-bit, the foggy cloud muffling the sounds of combat around me faded. The sheer volume of bodies lying around us should have made my gorge rise, but as it was, I could barely muster the interest.

When had we gotten up here?

I vaguely remembered getting to the stairwell and the fight there. The man holding me, swung around and stared. That was it—just *stared* at the guy rushing us. The guard switched directions abruptly and ran into a wall.

Not kidding. Slammed himself bodily into a wall, and the crunch of breaking bone hearkened back to Mad-Dragon's hallway snack.

Okay, that turned my stomach a little and had my pussy clenching.

Seriously, don't look at me like that. I said I was complicated.

"Like that, did you?" Fin asked, his lips against my ear. A delicious shiver worked its way down my spine. The guy looked like an angel and smelled like one. We might be surrounded by blood and gore, but pressed up to him, all I could scent was this deep, masculine flavor and something that reminded me of fresh brewed coffee. The perfect scent to start the day.

Fuck, I hadn't had coffee in weeks.

My hunger redoubled, and I nuzzled at his throat.

"Oh, so tempting, Beautiful," Fin chided with the faintest of groans. "But a little busy at the moment. Just hold that thought."

A familiar growl echoed behind me. "Don't you dare."

"Temper, temper. I told you she liked me best."

A dull roar echoed through the great stone chamber we were in. And really, it was huge. The ceiling stretched up at least three or four stories. Mad-Dragon could really stretch out in here.

"Trolls," Fin said abruptly, and Maddox swore. "A lot of trolls."

"What is it with you and trolls?"

"My sparkling personality?" Fin quipped. A giggle escaped, he was so blasé about it. Not all doom, gloom, and scowls like Maddox. Though to be perfectly fair, Maddox was hot.

Fin adjusted his stance, and I started to wiggle to have him put me down, but he gave my hip a squeeze.

"Stay put, Beautiful. We're going to get an opening any minute, and you're safer right where you are."

A pull, dark, luscious, and full of familiar lust tugged at me, and I snapped my head to the side.

Dorran.

The shadows around him thickened, and despite the herd of trolls storming toward us, it was Dorran who held all my focus. Hunger cramped my side, and I strained to pull away from Fin. The languidness weighing down my limbs evaporated. As much as the warden irked me, he could slake my thirst and quench my hunger.

"Fuck," Fin snapped. "Maddox get over here."

A growl reverberated as Maddox stepped into my line of sight, blocking Dorran. No, this wasn't right. I needed him. I didn't know this insane pair, and as charming as they might be—better the devil I knew.

The air around us darkened, even as Fin's grip on me turned to stone. He had my arms locked down, and the grip around my legs didn't let me do more than wiggle my feet. Not even the sweet attraction of his scent could dissuade me. A clash of bodies exploded in front of us as Maddox let loose with another roar.

Even though the twisting was in vain, I glared at Fin. Unfortunately, he ignored me in favor of narrowing his eyes at the troll looming over us. Maddox had vanished into the darkness, though the sounds of his battle roars and the collision of fleshy impacts added to the cacophony of battle. The troll bellowed with all of his stinky might, and the distraction loosened Fin's grip on me just enough to slip free.

He swore and then barely got his hands up in time to block the troll's huge and heavy fist. To my surprise, though really why *anything* surprised me at this point I couldn't say, Fin not only caught the monstrous arm that was easily thicker than his whole body, but he stopped it. Then struck with his own fist, sending the troll sliding backward.

Okay.

That was hot.

Astral-Boy had skills.

Fiona...

The whisper of Dorran's voice curved around me, and Fin's lovely face vanished as the shadows closed around me. Edging right up against pain and frustration, I turned into the darkness. It had never held any fear for me. My fingers had just brushed the warden's, when the darkness recoiled and a hard body slammed into me.

Bright light pierced the shadows, and my eyes watered at the burn. I hit the hard stone floor as the shadows whipped backwards, the tangle of them leaving me, and suddenly, all the throb of my shoulder head butted against the hunger pangs wrenching my sides, and I fucking hurt.

Seriously fucking hurt.

Legs obscured my view, and I canted my head back to find a Viking like figure standing over me. With hands that looked like they'd been dipped in blood and an expression so full of vicious wrath, he was a nightmare incarnate. Still, the warden retreated, even as tendrils of his darkness lashed out and slapped against the light, only to sizzle, pop, and burn.

I couldn't look away. It was kind of like staring into the sun during an eclipse. I was probably frying my retinas, but what was one more agony atop all the rest? A troll shrieked at the newcomer, and Viking-guy literally tore the guy in half and then ripped off one of his arms to beat another one.

"Well, better late than never," Fin said cheerfully as he hooked his hands under my armpits and dragged me upward. With my back against his chest, he bound me with his arms around me, even as...

"That's Rogue." The two disparate pieces of information snapped together like a puzzle slotting into place.

"Yup," Fin said, then nipped my ear. "We'll discuss you being shadow-addicted later, it's time to go."

The sting of his teeth scraping my earlobe sent an answering wave to all my other hurts. Somewhere along the way, I'd torn up my palms. There were gouges in my side that oozed blood, and I was pretty sure I'd bitten the inside of my lip. The blood welling up just added to my starvation.

Maddox emerged from the dust clouds and darkness, coated in gray ash with blood running in rivulets through it. Filthy, but alive.

It was a good look. Somewhere, he'd lost his shirt, but his pants held up despite being utterly shredded from one thigh down.

This was a man who could easily walk around in a loincloth and totally get away with it. To be honest, he should absolutely be encouraged.

Then the noise just kind of faded. Maddox stared at me, chest heaving and eyes furious. What the fuck did he have to be so pissed about? I wasn't the one who started all of this. If anything, I'd gotten dragged up those stairs.

Oh. Rescue effort.

Right.

I shook my head a little to try and clear more of the fog. Why it was so hard to focus all of a sudden, I didn't know. To be honest, it was like being drunk and fighting a hangover in the same breath, without any of the fun stuff—you know, like alcohol.

Our latest arrival spun, and if he wasn't a gruesome sight, I didn't know what was. The light around him had at least dimmed to not eye-popping bright anymore. But what held my attention now wasn't the gore on him or the light he'd extinguished, but the ferocity in those too blue eyes. They pinned me in place like an insect on a pegboard.

"He's been feeding on her," he said in a voice so rusty with disuse, it came out even deeper than Maddox's. "She won't leave willingly."

"We noticed," Fin stated almost idly. "Why do you think we've been trying to hang onto her?"

"Give her to me," Rogue ordered, but rather than release me, Fin actually backed up a step dragging me with him.

"Fight over her later," Maddox ordered. "We need to go now. The path is clear, but he'll bring back reinforcements."

"Let him," Rogue said with so much arrogance, I believed he would relish the opportunity. "Killing him would be one way to free her."

"While I don't mind the fight, I'd rather get Kitten to somewhere secure and let her feed. She's hungry."

Thank you.

I almost said it aloud, but then thought better of it when Rogue seemed intent on boring his way into my soul, and the longer he stared, the more uneasy I became.

Mad-Dragon I got.

Astral-Boy? Him, too. Mostly.

Even Dorran—longing punched through me. I'd been so close to feeding, and now he was absent. If I followed through with their insane plan, I'd be out of his reach.

That was what I wanted, right?

I wanted out of that cell.

Out of this prison.

I wanted what remnants of my life were left to me.

All of those things were true. But so was the sudden anxiety swarming me. If we left, I'd never see Dorran again. I might…

What, Fi? What might I do? Die?

The thought was so patently ridiculous, I snorted, and yet the ever tautening ball of anxiety in my chest began to compress my lungs.

"Give her to me," Rogue said taking a step toward us.

"No," Fin began, but whatever else he might have said was lost in a whoosh of motion as Rogue suddenly wrenched Fin's arms away from me and slid one of his gross, bloody hands to my waist. I slammed against him, and if Fin and Maddox were steely, Rogue was damn near diamond in his surface tension. No give. At all.

It was like being stabbed and cradled in equal measure.

Pleasure and pain.

His hunger?

It was absent.

Except…

The lust unfurled like a slow moving avalanche that gained force and speed as it rolled downward to me.

"I wasn't asking," Rogue finished his sentence, and then

the air whistled past us. I had to hold on for dear life and even managed to get my legs around his hips. He never so much as let me slip, but the wind hitting my back cut at me.

It must have sliced my shirt half to ribbons, or maybe that was my flesh. I barely had time to process Maddox's furious expression or Fin's shocked one before they were gone.

The race through the night seemed to stretch into infinity. Time ceased to have real meaning, and if not for the definitive squeeze of Rogue's hand to my ass, I might have written this off as a bad dream.

Nightmares. I had been known to have them.

I'd been stuck in one for weeks now. They even called it Nightmare Penitentiary.

The sudden stop would have cracked my neck, but Rogue had a hand against my hair. My gratitude for the thoughtfulness died a swift death when he pulled the hand away and my hair clung to the bloody debris decorating his fingers.

Yeah.

Gross.

Stomach lurching, I swallowed back the bile as the raw coppery scents from too many different bodies hit me at once. Troll. Shifter. Pretty sure a couple were vampires, too. And at least four or five others that I didn't know and really didn't want to know.

Instead of putting me down, Rogue pinned me to a wall and leaned his hips into mine. There was no heavy cock shoving its way at me, so that wasn't what he wanted.

Good—

The thought stuttered as he sliced at his throat just above where his neck joined his shoulder. Ancient blood slid out of the wound, fresh, hot, and so pungently sweet and savory, my mouth watered.

"Feed, little *sváss*." The order settled into my bones, and unlike Maddox or Fin, I wanted to obey this one even if a small part of me continued to rebel. I didn't even know this guy.

"I'm not a vampire," I argued.

"I don't care," he retaliated, and then cupped my head and pulled my mouth to the injury.

Yeah, that argument wasn't really working for me either.

The first brush of his blood to my lips, and I latched on without a second thought. Decadence exploded across my tongue, and I closed my eyes as a throaty moan vibrated in my throat.

Sinking my teeth into the wound, I worked it wider, and then it took active sucking to pull more blood from him. I applied myself, because I wanted more. Tightening my thighs against his hips, he rewarded every pull with a grind against me, and where he'd been lacking an erection before, one nudged at me now.

More, the crater of lust simmering beneath the surface cracked wide open, and then it swallowed me hole.

Fuck.

Me.

Maybe there was something to this vampire schtick.

CHAPTER 7

"'I don't believe in magic,' the young boy said. The old man smiled. 'You will when you see her.'" - Atticus

Fin

"*Droch chrích ort.*" Fin glared at the gaping hole in the wall through which Rogue vanished with their prize.

Maddox kicked a body away from him as he followed Fin's stare, then scowled at Fin.

"It's not my fault," Fin argued.

"No?" Maddox half-growled, half-rumbled. "Whose idea was it to bring him into the middle of this?"

"I stand by that idea." With a wave of his hand to the stacks of bodies around him, Fin paused, then pulled a hand-kerchief out of his inner pocket and began to clean the blood from his fingers as they made their way out. "It worked, didn't it?"

For his part, the surly dragon just grunted. "Where did he take her?"

Concentrating, Fin focused on the feel of his brother and where he might have gone. At the moment, there was a blankness to his presence. Out there, but just beyond perception. Rogue didn't want to be found immediately.

Probably protecting their prize. They'd only waited a few hundred years for her to be found, and the first word they get of her, she's trapped in a prison with a shadow demon feeding on her.

Not ideal.

Still…

The white square turned crimson as he continued cleaning his hands. They met no resistance as they made their way down the mountain. Finding vulnerable access points to the prison warded by magic and layered with the power of far too many dimensions to sit in just one had required all of Maddox's skills. Dragons kept their hoards in similar pockets, so he'd at least had a starting point.

Fin had been the one to confirm the vulnerability after Maddox located it. Maddox wasn't in a rush, if Fin didn't know better, he would suspect him of wanting the warden and his guards to pursue them here.

The prison might very well restore some of them. If they decided to follow, they wouldn't recover so easily if at all.

"Well?" Maddox demanded.

"He's blocking me at the moment." As much as he didn't want to admit it.

"Of course, he is. I made that woman a promise." The last came out through gritted teeth.

"How do you think I feel?" Fin turned it back on him. "She was supposed to sleep with me tonight." That, and she was hurting from lack of sustenance. The shadow addiction needed to be dealt with as well. Though Fin didn't doubt for an instant that Rogue couldn't handle her need to feed.

Conversation, on the other hand? Yeah, he wouldn't place any bets on that.

"He'd take her to the keep."

"No one goes to the keep anymore," Maddox argued. "We abandoned it fifty years after I turned."

"Which is why he would take her there."

Maddox understood hunting others, but he'd never had to hunt the rest of them. Why would he? They'd been friends, allies, and occasionally competitors for centuries. Time wore away the harsher edge of their disagreements, and they learned to seek each other out when they wanted the company and to ignore each other when they didn't. "Rogue always liked the keep. It's defensible. High in the mountains. We still own all of the land and the territory. It's never been developed. Urban expansionism won't reach there. The villages on the other side of the mountain are well tended and looked after. They have no reason to come looking for us."

There was another reason Rogue would have taken her there. If Maddox put away his rage for a few minutes, that would hit him, too.

"That's halfway around the world," he argued. "She was already weak."

"And craving," Fin confirmed. They were nearly a mile down the mountainside, and there was no sign of pursuit. A fact Maddox had obviously noticed as his agitation increased. "Rogue can feed her, *deartháir*. Even he understands how important it would be for a baby vamp to eat. His blood is older than ours."

"Not by much," Maddox snarled, but some of the heat drained from his tone, and the scorching air around them cooled. "*If* he took her there..."

"He did." Of that much, Fin was certain.

"You think he's going to try and wake Alfred."

"I would," Fin admitted, and Maddox glared at him. "Look, Alfred went to sleep because the world had worn him out. He'd tired of waiting. We were as safe as we could be, and we didn't need him to look after us. But when he went to ground, Rogue..." Rogue turned away from them.

Even when Fin would try to lure him out, Rogue never stayed. He always came. He'd never let them down, not once. But when he finished his task, he vanished again. Try as he might, Fin hadn't been able to keep him with them. Maddox no longer bothered and acted like it was a crime to even try and lure Rogue out of his self-imposed exile.

"She isn't ready for Alfred."

"I doubt she's ready for any of us," Fin said with a shrug. "It's our job to protect her and make her ready. Besides, she's got spunk. You're already a little crazy about her, aren't you?"

Never had he been so jealous of and thrilled for the dragon in equal measure. Fiona MacRieve was the answer to so much. All they had to do was save her from the insanity of vampire politics, keep the shadow demon away, and show her that being a hybrid was destiny.

"She's a stubborn wench," Maddox grunted. "Fierce, too. I could live without her need to fuck the stupid out of people."

Eyebrows raised, Fin eyed him. "She needed to feed, and I don't think she planned to hop on and ride the guys."

"The shadow demon's been fucking her."

"Well, that was before she met us." Fin kept it philosophical. They'd hardly been monks. Well, Maddox might have been, there was no telling with him. He didn't share much, and Alfred probably wouldn't know a date if it woke up and bit him. Rogue? Yeah, Fin wouldn't place money there either.

Fine, Fin hadn't been a monk.

Course, if the warden had been paying her visits, that would explain the shadow addiction. They could keep her away until they cleansed her system.

"You up for transporting two of us?" Maddox asked abruptly, and Fin didn't bother to hide his smirk.

"Already eager to see her again?"

"I made her a deal," Maddox gritted out. "She'd listen to the whole story, then she was free to go if she wanted."

"That's a terrible deal, why would you offer her that?" Fin stared at him.

"Because she wants nothing to do with us, and she's still fighting the fact she was turned. She needs a sense of control." Then Maddox gave him a firm look. "I plan on honoring my word."

Of course, he did.

Dragons had honor for miles. Sometimes for days.

Why had the species begun to die out? Oh right, they *honored* their treaties when so many others didn't.

"Well, good for us, I made no such promises." He clapped Maddox's shoulder and then focused. Inside him, the magic unlocked. Portal magic wasn't difficult. If anything, it was one of the first mysteries he'd trained in as a young druid. Trees linked the world, their root systems tangling deep beneath the earth and creating routes that those who developed the art could slip along.

Even when a tree had been uprooted, the memory of its pathways remained, which meant even wooden structures couldn't keep him out if he could find the right one. It was knowing how to read the myriad of pathways and follow them. Taking passengers along was slightly more difficult.

But only slightly.

Maddox didn't block him out as he wrapped his power around him. If anything, the dragon allowed Fin access to his own strength, not that this simple transport required it. The world whooshed past them as he found the route they needed and followed it home.

Coinnigh an Rí, King's Keep, had been the center of

Alfred's domain for years beyond counting. They'd all called it home at one point or another. Granted, it was a monolith built almost completely from cut stones hauled miles from their natural habitat and put together.

Magic infused some of the stones, but the rest of it? They'd held it with strength, skill, and wit. When that wasn't enough, a few good slaughters had at least been entertaining. The factions left them alone. But they'd begun to fade from common memory. A choice, really, if the majority didn't think about them, they didn't have to fend off the occasional glory seeker.

The problem, however, was the reckoning Fiona faced. The turning of other species besides human into a vampire was considered impossible, improbable, and socially unacceptable. The legends around so-called hybrids had painted them as monsters.

Well, at least they got that part right.

While rare, hybrids existed in a delicate balance. One Fin, Maddox, Rogue, and Alfred maintained. They were all hybrids. Some of the first.

Currently, the only ones beyond Fiona.

They'd waited a long time for her.

Too long.

Whisking along the paths, he slowed them as they neared the ancient oaks bordering the fields nearest the keep's location. With a pop, he stepped out and yanked Maddox with him. The dragon looked vaguely green, and Fin chuckled as he patted him once and left him to catch his breath. It was a testament to how much Maddox wanted to see *her* again that he'd not objected to transporting on the ancient pathways.

He preferred to fly, but the keep was halfway around the world from where they'd penetrated Nightmare Penitentiary's defenses. It would have taken him a while to get there, and that meant leaving the beautiful Fiona to Fin and Rogue.

Huh. Maybe he should have let Maddox fly on his own.

The sight of smoke curling toward the sky from one of the chimney flues had Fin smirking. He smacked Maddox's arm again. "See, I told you he would bring her here."

The defenses were still active, but they had nothing to worry about. They passed harmlessly through the magical field that would send up an alarm to them no matter where they were of possible invasion. Once inside, Fin took a cleansing breath.

It had been a long time since he'd come home. The air was cool and damp, but the clouds had already parted to let watery sunshine reach the wet earth. They'd just missed the rain. While it had been night where they made their escape, it was nearly midday here.

The wood smoke was almost an invitation to a fire roaring in one of the man-sized hearths that decorated the halls. In the old days, there would be casks of ale and pots of honeyed mead. The food and drink would be free flowing. Artists and musicians often brought in from far and wide would provide the entertainment before Fin left them with pleasant memories and they were sent on their way, purses laden with coin.

The good old days.

Course, now they had internet and access to all types of entertainment at the press of a button. But there wasn't wi-fi up here.

He'd have to fix that if they settled in for the next few decades while Fiona adjusted. The main doors groaned as Maddox got ahead of him and pushed them open. Heavy steel doors needed a winch for most to open, but they weren't so similarly burdened. Inside, he gave Maddox a hand in shutting them both.

Memories echoed against the walls, filling the silence with images from other times. How many times had Alfred shoved these great doors open to allow his men to enter? How often had Rogue followed right in his shadow, a silent sentinel? At times, Fin and Maddox had also been there, always welcome. A brotherhood formed out of necessity, unity, and transition. They were the only ones of their kind to survive.

"The baths." Maddox's words seemed to hang in the air as he vanished. The disturbed dust marked his passage. Fin followed at a more sedate pace. Like Maddox, he was also eager to see Fiona again. He'd only gotten to hold her for a brief time. Clouding her mind to ease her compliance for their flight had backfired when the shadow demon arrived.

In the future, Fin wouldn't make that mistake again.

Ascending the stairs, he followed the sound of the water. The old boilers and piping through the walls used a system of cisterns and aqueducts built through the mountain itself to bring fresh water in, heat it, and then fill the pools in the bathing chamber. That, along with fires laid at each end, made it the warmest and steamiest room in the keep.

It had been the height of convenience hundreds of years earlier, and he couldn't say he would mind a bath himself. Blood had dried on his skin and left him itchy.

Maddox's aggravated voice tickled at his ears as Fin followed the long hall toward the bathing rooms. The bedrooms were all on the floor above, and while hot baths could be pulled there, the old bathhouse idea had still been popular when Alfred settled the keep.

Stripping off his coat, Fin let himself into the oversized chamber. Five pools placed strategically around the room with varying levels to each pool afforded bathers with a place to wash, a place to soak, and a place to steam by ascending the levels.

Unsurprisingly, Fiona was sprawled in a soaker pool, her arms hooked against the sides as she half-floated. Her eyes were closed and expression blissful. Across from her, Rogue sat, naked and cleaned. His dirty blond hair had been recently washed and hung halfway down his back. He flicked his gaze at Fin as he approached the pool.

Like Rogue, Fiona was also naked, but she didn't seem remotely aware of them. Flushed with color, her gorgeous red hair clung to her skin, though in places, it had begun to curl away. The tips of her breasts were just barely visible. While Fin looked forward to exploring her with great detail, he focused on the necessities for the moment.

The vicious bite in her shoulder was almost closed, the angry black lines radiating out from it the last bits of venom being decimated by her body.

"Why the fuck did you just take her?" Maddox demanded. Not waiting for Rogue to answer, he continued, "I had a deal with her. She would hear us out, then if she chose to go, I wouldn't stop her."

Lifting a flask, Rogue took a long drink, then held it out to Maddox wordlessly. The dragon scowled and accepted it.

"Fin shouldn't have dragged you into it, we had it covered." He took a long pull from the flask himself, then passed it back before he stripped off his own clothes and sank down into the lower pool. The water went crimson and streaked as the blood, dust, and soot worked free of his skin. "The point," he persisted. "You weren't aware of the rest of the plan, and you just kidnapped her. That completely contravenes *my* word. Now I have to make up for that lost honor."

Fin met Rogue's bemused gaze, and the other just shrugged. Unfortunately for Maddox, neither Fin nor Rogue shared his honor system.

Nor had they made her any promises. Well, Fin had more or less suggested his word in getting her out.

"You fed her?" he checked with Rogue. The blond nodded

once, then motioned to his throat. There was a fading wound there, likely inflicted by himself. Breaking his skin was damn hard and many had tried.

Crouching, Fin used careful fingers to tilt her head to look at her throat. No other bite marks marred her skin saved for the one faded scar that would likely always remain. The mark of her maker. Lashes lifting, she stared up at him with ruby colored eyes, though they weren't as blood-red as they'd been when he found her and Maddox in the hall. The barest hint of green surrounded them.

"Hmm, getting better at that astral projection," she murmured.

He chuckled. "Rest, Beautiful." He punched just a bit of compulsion into the command, and she let out a sigh, head tipped back and throat vulnerable as she sank under again. Yeah, that wouldn't hold.

Maddox growled at him. "Don't take advantage."

"Actually, I'm just making sure she's in one piece and doesn't try to escape on us before I've had a bath. Just because you need to chain women up to get them to stick around, doesn't mean I have to."

Rogue snorted, but the weight of Maddox's cold stare was even more impressive than his growls. Tossing a glance toward him, Fin gave him a little chin dip. Some lines weren't worth crossing.

Hardly mollified, the dragon went back to his bath, and Fin finally stepped down to shed his own blood-marked and shredded clothing. The fight had been impressive. They'd mustered their defenses, but it was hard to take on a druid and a dragon individually, much less together. Throw in a warrior, and they were really outmatched.

When the king awoke…

Fin paused, eyes closing for a moment as he searched the keep mentally. Alfred hadn't stirred yet. There was no mistaking his influence once he left his sleep. It was a crackle of energy in the air, a weight that draped everything, his power and his protection. The absence of it was just as keen.

They had so much to show him when he did rouse. The world would fascinate him. At least it had gotten interesting since the last time he was awake, anyway.

The water stung Fin's skin as he slid into it. The temperature higher than the air around them, Maddox had already moved up to sit in the soaking pool. Fin ducked himself into the water, then scrubbed the last flakes of blood and debris off. Having spent hours tucked under a stone floor, he could use the scrub.

Finished, he ascended and settled into the hotter water. Rogue turned a bland eye on him, then nodded toward Fiona.

Her closed eyes and serene expression were not something Fin wanted to disturb. "It can wait," he said quietly.

Maddox scowled.

"She's exhausted. All of our intelligence says she was dumped there within hours of her first waking. I can't imagine transitioning in there was very easy."

"No," Maddox admitted as he wrapped an arm around her and pulled her against his side. She let out a little sound that Fin swore was a purr. Her lashes moved faintly, and then she seemed to recognize Maddox and curled right up against him.

Jealousy painted bloody stripes through him, especially when Maddox's expression turned smug. Yeah, she was probably sleeping with Maddox again that night.

Fine.

Fin would lure her away the next day.

"Don't fight," Rogue ordered, and Fin wasn't the only one who jerked a look to the silent sentinel. The fact that he'd spoken at all when he took Fiona from the prison had been a collection of more words than they'd heard from him in a long time. At his quizzical look, Rogue shrugged. "If you fight over her, I'll end her."

Fin blinked and Maddox scowled, his arms closing around her, and between one blink and the next, it was the dragon staring at Rogue. If he worried about the dragon's rage, the other didn't show it.

"We didn't wait all these years for her for you to just throw that out there," Fin argued, choosing his words carefully. "We're not fighting."

"You're jealous, and he's possessive." Rogue didn't sound like he cared, but it would be a mistake to believe he was cavalier. If he truly didn't give a damn, he wouldn't even be broaching the topic. To Maddox, Rogue said, "You hate that she fed from me and that she is replete because I made sure to give her enough."

The dragon still scowled, but the recrimination seemed to turn inward.

Not to leave him out, Rogue switched his attention to Fin. "You resent she already has comfort with him. You want to claim what he's already found."

"You're not wrong," Fin agreed. "But I can be jealous because I want to know her, too. I've dreamt about her for centuries. Unlike the rest of you, I knew she was coming. I never broke faith."

"Lust-filled dreams about her breasts are not what I would call prophetic," Maddox stated drily, and Rogue gave a half-laugh.

"Oh, if I'd dreamed about those tits, trust me, I'd have found her a whole lot sooner." As it was, the little succubus hadn't even been on his radar until the day she awoke changed. Then the whole world had seemed to ring with her presence. He couldn't not leave immediately on a quest to find her.

The mental anguish alone would have drawn him like a beacon, but it was the raw and primal fury that kept him on target. He'd arrived a day after the sense of her all but muted. It had only taken him interrogating a half-dozen vampires in Dallas to find out where she'd gone.

He knew the name of her maker. The vampire was in hiding at the moment. When he brought his head above ground, Fin would deliver it to her on a platter. Though in truth, they owed him—it was a bumbling and idiotic attempt on the vampire's part to try and turn her in the first place.

By all rights, it should have killed her.

Fiona let out a little sigh. "You know, if you want to talk and keep me awake, you could discuss something more interesting than my breasts. Like, why I'm here and what this great plan was that I had to listen to before I could take off?"

With a slow shake of his head, Rogue slid down into the water. "You need more rest."

The fact that he addressed her directly sent Maddox's eyebrows skyward, even as Fin raised his own.

"Uh huh," Fiona elongated the two syllables even as she stretched. The action shifted her away from Maddox and brought her glorious breasts above the water. They really were quite spectacular. While slighter than he generally preferred in his women, Fiona's curves might also be lacking because of her half-starved state. The denial of her nature and her reliance on a shadow demon meant she might be alive, but she wasn't as healthy as she could be.

Rogue's blood had made a great deal of difference.

"Look," she continued, glancing from Rogue to Fin and finally to Maddox. Fin was almost disappointed he hadn't rated a longer look. Almost. Though the narrowing of her sleepy eyes gave her a harsher appearance. "We had a deal, right, Mad-Dragon?"

"We did," Maddox confirmed, not even batting an eyelash at what she called him. "I have not forgotten, Kitten."

"Good. I'd hate to think of you as an oath breaker. But we're going to put a little clock on this. I've been stuck in a cell for weeks, and this girl has places to go and people to kill. So let's cut to the chase. Why did you bust me out of that place, and what is it you're expecting in payment?"

"No payment would ever be asked," Fin told her smoothly. It had been their privilege to retrieve her, and pleasure. Or at least, it would be to all their pleasure.

"Wasn't asking you, Astral-Boy," she retorted, though the flash of her glance in his direction had him sitting up. "Though you are pretty, I will give you that."

He grinned.

"But I was talking to tall, dark, and ruthless over here." She jerked her thumb at Maddox.

Rogue chuckled.

"What are you laughing at?" Fin demanded, but the blond lifted his hands, palms out, as if saying not his problem.

With a sigh, Fin focused on Fiona, but she stared at Maddox and his dragon stared back at her.

"You're a hybrid," Maddox said finally, almost reluctantly. "You were right when you said vampires cannot turn other supernaturals, right in as much as that's all current thought holds to it. However, what they know and what is fact are two vastly different things."

Fiona stared at him for a bit, her lips pursed. Keen intelligence flickered in her eyes as she studied him. "So I'm a vampire-succubus."

"Yes."

"I need to feed on lust and blood."

"Also yes."

"Well. Aren't I special?"

"Very," Fin exhaled. "More special than you realize."

"Oh? And how is that?"

Ignoring Maddox's warning look, Fin told her the truth. "You're the only female hybrid to ever transition. You're also ours. Our mate. Perfect for us in every way." And she was.

Maddox sighed, even as Rogue just shook his head, but Fiona's response puzzled him the most.

She burst out laughing.

"Oh, honey, I'm a succubus," she said in between gasps. "I'm pretty much perfect for everyone."

Oh.

Fin hadn't really thought of it that way, and the dark look on Maddox's face promised he had, but it was the speculation filling Rogue's expression that worried him all of a sudden.

Wiping at her eyes, Fiona shook her head. "Sorry, I just needed that laugh. Like I said, Astral-Boy, you really are pretty. But you shouldn't bet on me. As soon as this little confab is over, I'm out of here. Like I said, places to go and people to kill." The she muttered something about how destiny could bite her.

"We'll see," he murmured, even as Maddox let out an aggrieved sigh.

"You will need to stay with us long enough to master your bloodlust," Maddox informed her. "And until we can deal with your sire. You do not want him to try and control you."

From the look on her face, Fiona had no intentions of letting anyone control her.

But she might have missed the point. Destiny had already bitten *all* of them. But as long as they were naked, he didn't mind the argument at all.

It would help when they got to the makeup part.

Which they would need in three…

Two…

"I don't care what Maddox promised you," Rogue stated. "You're not leaving, little *sváss*."

Now.

Her eyes flashed, and Maddox growled.

Fin settled back against the ledge to soak and let Maddox and Rogue debate this one.

Then Fin could swoop in with the reasonable compromise and settle it all.

When she stood up abruptly, hands on her hips, he damn near swallowed his tongue.

She really was quite perfect.

And it didn't matter if everyone else wanted her.

They didn't get to have her.

Fiona was theirs.

CHAPTER 8

"I don't believe in love at first sight. You fall in lust with what your eyes see, and in love with what your heart sees." - Unknown

*M*aybe it was the amount of blood I'd consumed or the age of it, but focusing had become a real bitch. What had been promised as a conversation and explanation had turned into a dictation and argument.

Specifically, Maddox argued, Rogue dictated, and Fin leaned back, arms stretched out, looking enormously satisfied. A certain amount of smugness rolled off Astral-Boy, and fuck, he was so pretty. I'd be jealous, but I wasn't that shallow.

I also really didn't give a damn about beauty except to admire it. Maddox was ripped, powerful, and yes, the fact that he could turn into a dragon was really impressive. But he wasn't *pretty*. Strong. Fierce. Proud. These all applied. Handsome, in his own way, but no, Fin had pretty all tied up.

"You can't just give her that order," Maddox snarled. It was really sweet, and I should probably calm him down, but to be honest, I didn't really care what *Rogue* had decided. The fact that he'd tasted divine and fed me both his blood and his lust had left me floating. He hadn't turned it into sex, not that I'd been remotely opposed, despite the varying levels of grossness decorating both of us. And by that, I meant him, not me. I did not look or *smell* anywhere near that bad.

But the stoic male sitting across the hot bath—really, these weren't baths so much as actual pools, and they were more like hot rock tubs. While they were carved out of actual stone, they were smooth and comfortable. Maddox kept trying to settle me back into leaning against him even if I didn't want to sit yet. Finally, I sat because it was warmer *in* the water. When he tugged me against him again I elbowed him.

Hated to let him know he wasn't any softer than the rocks we sat against. Not that I examined why I was loath to let him know. Anyway, back to the stoic over there.

Him, I couldn't pin down. Fierce? Yes. Beautiful? In a cold and kind of deadly way. There was an ancient power lurking there, something that might possibly be more dangerous than the dragon at my side.

Maybe.

That?

That was sexy as fuck.

"I think I just did," Rogue replied, his tone serene. He just did what? Oh, right. Gave me an order. "If you didn't want her, you wouldn't have gone into the prison in the first place. You wouldn't have given them the chance to shackle you."

"They can't hold me." Maddox glanced at me. "They wouldn't be able to hold me, and I wouldn't let them keep you. This is not something you need to concern yourself about."

"Are you talking to me or to tall, blond, and tasty over there?"

Maddox opened his mouth to respond, then paused, a puzzled look sliding through his expression before he finally said, "His name is Rogue."

"Yeah, I'm all caught up on that part, not that I care." I slanted a look toward the god lounging in the water. "Not that I don't appreciate the fact you got me off and fed me. Seriously enjoyed that. No lie."

"You're welcome. I take guesting seriously. You will not go hungry while you are here." Well, that was *almost* sweet. "You will be here for a while." That was not.

Eyes narrowed, I studied him. "Maddox and I had a deal."

"Exactly," Maddox stated, slinging an arm around me. Now, while I wasn't opposed to the skin on skin contact, I also wasn't interested in the distraction right now. "I gave her my word."

"I didn't," Rogue stated, as though that ended the discussion.

"Fin," Maddox snarled.

"Sorry, big guy," Fin said without opening his eyes, and a smile curved his lips. "I'm on Rogue's side in this. I didn't give her my word either. I said we'd get her out. Which we did. I said we'd feed her, which Rogue has handled this evening." Those beautiful brown eyes opened, and he latched his heated gaze onto me. "FYI, I'll be helping out with the feeding, too. It will be easier on you if you just feed from all of us."

Easier on me. Well that was mighty damn *autocratic* of him and probably had nothing to do with the want in his eyes.

"You know," I drawled sliding away from the dragon. Dragon.

Fuck me.

Yeah, focus.

Rising from the steaming water, I moved toward the side.

"You should soak for a little while longer," Fin suggested. "You're still buzzing from feeding."

And you're fighting the bliss.

The fact that his words flashed against the inside of my mind had me turning. Searching for his access point, I focused on pushing him back out. He studied me with the most patient of puzzled frowns.

Harmonics I'd learned young danced through my mind. One perk of being well-fed, I was also well-armed.

A vampiric succubus. It was an oxymoron.

Elias was going to kill me.

"Who would Elias be?" Fin asked. The sudden resonance of three gazes slamming into me had me rolling my eyes. "Because you can forget him along with Dorran."

Unimpressed, I chuckled. "Elias falls into the category of 'none of your fucking business,'" I informed him. "And Dorran kept me alive."

"Dorran is a the name the shadow demon gave you?" Unlike Fin's playful tone or Maddox's near constant growl, Rogue's voice was more indolent, but power crackled in every syllable. This was not a being who tolerated being ignored.

What he was precisely, I hadn't figured out yet.

Vampires.

Hybrids.

Oh, and how had Fin put it? My mates.

I snorted. Folding my arms, I leaned against the side. The air above the water was much cooler, and goosebumps rippled over my skin and turned my nipples taut. It was a good reminder that I wasn't here for sex and games.

You could be... Fin's teasing remark stroked across my mind like a caress. Bad vampire. I slapped his mental fingers with a slam of shutting off his access. The harmonics kept witches out of my head. One perk to having known a witch singer, those same harmonics kept other magic users out, too.

He gave a little jerk of surprise, his lazy air dissipating as he stared at me with blown pupils. "That... How did you do that?"

"Ask me no questions, and I'll tell you no lies," I chastised him.

Maddox snarled, "Stop poking in her head. We're supposed to be convincing her, not chasing her away."

Well, that was useful knowledge.

"I was playing," Fin argued. "Besides, she thinks I'm pretty. So suck it."

The corner of my mouth kicked up as Maddox surged to his feet, his glare fixed on Fin. There was something really— the thought didn't finish because the icy air around me sucked all the breath out of me. The bathing room was gone as were the sexy brutes about to argue over me.

I barely had time to process Rogue's hands on me before he dropped me in the middle of a bed in a dark, really fucking cold room. My teeth chattered before I could stop them.

"Stay," he ordered with a single gesture in my direction. Like me, he was still naked but the cold—fuck, were we in Siberia?—didn't seem to affect him. Or maybe he was just a better actor. Crossing the room, he moved a flap then struck a match. The smell of sulphur tinged the air, and a minute later, a fire bloomed in the hearth. It wasn't quite as large as the huge furnaces he called fireplaces in the bathing room, but the heat licked at the icy air around us.

"Do I look like a dog?" At least a plume of dust hadn't floated up into the air when I hit the comforter. Speaking of which, the fabric was softer than any I'd felt in days.

"You look like exactly what you are," Rogue informed me

as he lifted a heavy blanket from a chest and carried it over toward me. It wasn't just a blanket…it was a fur.

He snapped it out, and the wash of icy air sent a shudder down my spine. The fur settled over me like a heavy cloud. A heavy *warm* cloud. My still damp hair didn't offer much warmth, but tracing the way the water droplets slid down his skin seemed to be plenty of distraction. When we'd been in the bath, I hadn't really paid attention to the black ink scrawled over his skin or the patterns it made.

"I'm sure there's an insult in there somewhere," I murmured, skimming my gaze down to the half-hard cock stirring despite the brittle cold. Even though I expected it, when he slid beneath the fur with me, surprise still skated along my flesh. "What I'm uncertain about is whether you're trying to offend me or…"

Undeterred by my comments, he levered across the bed, shifting the fur to drape both of us, and then he dragged my legs apart.

Really, like just gripped and spread. With one tug, he had me on my back and his shoulders wedged between my thighs. "Fiona," he said, staring up at me with eyes gone shimmering blue. "Shut up."

"Excuse you?"

My next thought completely stuttered however as his hot breath passed right over my pussy to the inside of my thigh and then his teeth sank in. Rage kindled in my blood, but desire stomped right over it as his lust boiled over again. Lust to taste me, to feed himself, and to fuck me.

As full as I already was, his wild need shouldn't be pounding into my veins and taking over my pulse. Not that I was even remotely struggling against his hold.

What? I liked dominant men. Especially those who just went for what they wanted. It beat the hell out of the guys who tried to *lure* me in with pretty promises.

The hot pull of his mouth seemed to absorb all my focus, and with every tug, there was an answering pulse in my pussy. Fuck. I was going to be soaked in no time. I clenched at the blanket or the sheets. Anything to hang on because the orgasm he sent crashing through me shattered any arguments.

Two fingers—stiff like marble but hot like lava—speared into me, and I wanted to roll my hips and ride, but his fierce grip kept my lower body still, impaled and pinned beneath fingers and fangs. Toes curling, I dug them against his back as he sucked down more, and the vibrant buzz along my flesh doubled, then redoubled until he crooked his fingers and I came again.

The wrench of reality faded as I floated on a sea of sensation with his hot need sizzling into my soul. I was almost too full, I couldn't consume more, and yet, more was what I got. Still, he continued to suck, pulling and draining me. Feeding one beast, he starved the other.

The lazy seal of his tongue stroking the bite mark sent little eddies of fresh pleasure through me. His fingers were still sheathed in my pussy, even as my inner walls fluttered and clenched against them.

"Better," he murmured before he began to lick along the seam of my labia. Blood loss left me pliant. He hadn't drained me completely, but weakness invaded my limbs as he began to suck against my clit. The storm that unleashed made me twitch.

"Much better," he continued as the room flashed from color to black and white, then back again. Everything was hazy. "You have two natures," he informed me as he tugged his fingers free from my pulsating flesh, and I whimpered.

Fucking. Whimpered.

Oh. Hell. No.

Even as I rejected the need swelling through me, I couldn't deny the pleasure still quaking under my skin.

"They both need to be fed," he continued lazily before he latched onto a nipple and began to suck. The sting of his teeth came a second later, and he began to drink again. The haze at the edge of my vision darkened further.

How much was he going to take? The errant thought drifted through my mind, but couldn't light or take purchase. A lick and a kiss, then he was at my throat, and the drag of his chest rasped against my nipples, twining pain and pleasure.

Hovering above me, he nestled his hips against mine, even as he slid a hand down to grip my thigh and drag it upward. "Now," he murmured, his breath hot against my lips. "You need to feed."

"Asshole," I whispered. "I didn't need it before you did that."

"No," he said, simply. "You need it more than you know. The shadow demon fed on you constantly, Fiona. He chomped away at pieces of your soul, pieces you could restore because you fed on him."

So? But the challenge died unspoken.

"And he's going to call you because his blood is in you."

I almost laughed. "Pretty sure it's in you…" His cock teased at my entrance, and it wasn't half-hard anymore. No, it was thicker and far stiffer than his fingers had been. Rogue didn't kiss me, though his nose brushed mine. Licking my lips, I fought the gradual darkening of my vision. "I fed on you once," I argued.

"Yes, and you're going to do it again," Rogue ordered. "You'll feed on all of us. We're going to feed on you until we clean him out of you."

I laughed. My fangs grazed against the inside of my lips as I smiled. "Demanding fucker, aren't you?"

With one hand, he clamped it against my chin. "Tell me your objections."

"To being fucked?" I shrugged. "Not many. Though a girl does like to be asked before she's thrown on a bed in an icy room and tongued to orgasm. Or in your case…" I licked my lips again. "Fanged and fingered."

He chuckled. "You don't want to be asked."

No, I really didn't.

"You just don't want to be a vampire."

Nope. I didn't want that either.

"But you are."

Asshole.

"More, you're a hybrid."

Yeah, I got that. Flicking my gaze from him, I stared at the shadowed ceiling.

"How did he feed you, little *sváss*?"

What the fuck was a *sváss*?

"Tell me," he commanded.

"Blood bags were how they tried." It was an answer without being an answer.

His fingers tightened against my jaw in warning. His cock nestled right against my labia, the tip pressing against my clit, but his absolute lack of motion meant if I wanted anything more I'd have to grind.

Well, two could play the denial game, fuck you very much. I might not have the strength to move after he bit me so intensely—that had felt ridiculously good—but he didn't control me.

No one controlled me.

"Disgusting."

I glanced back up to find those too blue eyes still glowing as he stared at me. "Agreed."

"You didn't drink from them?"

I would have shaken my head, but I couldn't move it.

Okay, the restraint game had potential, but this was getting old. His lust still licked over me, fanning against my bloated soul like I needed more, and fuck if I wasn't absorbing it. It wasn't quite enough to edge the need above empty where his draining had left me.

"But you drank from the demon?"

"Don't judge me."

Rogue snorted. "I'm not. I'm judging them. Did you drink from the demon or not?"

I shrugged as much as I was able. I'd half-expected Fin or Maddox to have tracked me down by now, but apparently not. Maybe I wasn't even in Castle Numbskull or wherever it was Rogue had dragged me off to.

"Are you planning to fuck me or just interrogate me?"

"Feeling restless, little *sváss*?" He ran his nose along my cheek to my throat. My heart clenched at the first scrape of his teeth. Fight surged into my veins. If he wanted to bite my thighs or my breasts, fine. I didn't want him at my throat. Strength surged through me, and I reached for the lust he had on simmer.

One beautiful thing about being a succubus, I might feed on lust, but I could also fan it. While I had no idea what the hell Rogue was in addition to being a vampire, three facts were distinctly clear.

He was a vampire.

He was old.

He was *very* male.

His cock stiffened further at the first surge hitting his system. He snapped his head up and his teeth away from my throat. The flare of his nostrils and the shift in his eyes told me that I'd found the right circuit.

"*Sváss*," he warned me. Jaw clenched, he ground his hips into mine, and the slide of his cock against my clit threatened my concentration, but I just added that fuel to the fire. A shudder overcame him, then another. "You should stop."

"You first," I pointed out. I wasn't the one who threw my naked ass on this bed and went down on me without so much as a *may I*. I wasn't the one who kidnapped me out of a prison—granted, I was glad to be out, but I refused to trade one cell and keeper for another.

Rogue began to shake, but his grip on me didn't loosen. When his eyes flared from blue to pure white, it was my turn to shiver. Nothing natural inhabited that brilliant gaze of pure white light. The shadows in the room retreated, and even the glow from the fire seemed insignificant in comparison to the pure light escaping him.

"What are you?" I had to ask.

"Dangerous," he replied, and then his mouth clamped down on mine and all that power surged back into me. My lust. His. Like a feedback loop, and I stopped squirming to wrap my arms around him. At some point, he fisted his cock and then pushed into me, and I dragged my other leg up until I had them both locked around his hips.

The piston of his hips slamming into mine should have brought pain, but fuck, it was exactly what I needed and wanted. He filled me with every thrust, the friction generating more heat if possible, until what breath escaped his punishing kiss fogged in the air. His tongue matched his cock for lashes inside my mouth, and I dug my nails into his shoulders. When he ripped his mouth upward, his whole expression was one of tortured need, and I didn't shy from it, arching up to meet the rock of his hips.

The feel of him working through me lit me up. Fucking and I were old friends, but this was different. This was... I couldn't hold on to the spiraling thought. When he yanked out of me, I hissed, but the fur fell away as he rose up on his knees and slammed me back when I would have followed him. I got one brief glance at his cock, straining out toward me, thick, curved, and seeming to pulsate.

Oh, mama was intrigued. With one grip of my legs, he flipped me over onto my stomach and dragged my hips up. When he impaled me again, I didn't bother to hold back the scream or the need to claw at the covers. He wrapped my hair around his fist and anchored one hip with his hand, and then he began to drive every thought out of my head.

The flood of lust filling me redoubled, and I had to send it back to him. His cock seemed to swell, and it took real effort for him to work it into me over and over again. Every drag and push against my pussy lit me up more, and when he yanked me up and back, then slid his hand down to flick my clit, I came apart. His teeth sank into my throat, and his own orgasm flooded me as he roared.

Life suspended on a rocky precipice, pleasure and pain pulling me taut as raw power filled me until it spilled over, leaving only bliss as he pumped inside of me and drained me at the same time.

The world splintered, and I sank into a haze of pure pleasure.

"Fuck," Maddox's voice weaved through the brilliant darkness holding me. "Stop."

I wasn't doing anything, just riding out orgasm after orgasm as it detonated in my system. My clit hurt, Rogue had teased it so much at this point, and yet even that pain sent eddies of pleasure to drown me. The darkness pulled me down.

"I said *stop.*" The roar punched down to me and dragged me back to the surface.

Dragon.

Right.

Then hot hands were on my face, and another mouth claimed mine. Where Rogue tasted like ice, Maddox was all fire. The heat flamed through me, even as ice coated my back. The bruising force of Rogue's grip was still in my hair and skating along my chest to my breasts, and despite his own orgasm, he was still thick and buried deep.

Some distant part of my mind wondered at the fact he could still stretch me so tight.

"Feed her," another voice penetrated the floating haze. "I can't believe he fucking drained her." Fin.

Right. Astral-Boy was there.

Astral-Boy.

Dragon.

Wild Dick.

Yeah, that last name really applied because I wanted to rock against that dick still impaling me, and at the same time, I wanted to feel him moving again. What did it say about me that I wanted this sexy combo of desire and torture?

"Kitten," Maddox said in a harsh voice, and cupped my face. The weight of his thumbs worked my mouth wider. "You need to feed."

"Oh…" I husked out another laugh as fresh lust crashed into me. I was feeding. The words weren't forming. My tongue was too thick…

"You asshole," Maddox snarled. Not really the way to romance a lady, but I didn't have it in me to care. "What the hell were you thinking?"

"He's lust drunk, what do you think he was thinking?" Fin snapped. "Just feed her. He's all knotted up inside her and not moving for a while."

Oh, that was nice. I was now a glorified cock warmer.

"Drink," Maddox urged me in a much softer voice. Better.

He cupped my head, straining against the hand already wrapped in my hair, and my breasts impacted his hot chest. Oh. Sandwich. Then blood trickled against my lips, and I swallowed.

Sweet.

Hot.

Spicy.

I latched on to the slender cut and worked it wider. If Rogue had been decadence, Maddox was pure gratification. The tingling in my lips spread down my throat as he both quenched the raw emptiness and set it on fire. I clutched at him, moaning as I drank more, and he swore again. Every gulp had me clenching, and Rogue let out a strangled groan.

"Fuck," Fin whispered, and really, what could I do but agree?

Maddox kept my face planted to his throat, and I writhed between him and Rogue, glutting myself on the blood and pleasure they offered.

Behind me, Rogue finally loosened and slipped away. The chill at my back when he released me had me shaking. Then Maddox forced my head up and away, and I growled.

Actually growled. I wanted more.

"Shh, Beautiful." Fin had his arms around me, and then he tucked my face to his throat and the scent of his blood hit me. Forests and sunlight and sumptuous spring days, and I clamped down on the cut waiting for me. An orgasm shattered me even as I fed, and what few splinters of the world I'd held onto slid right through my fingers.

"Why the fuck did you do that?" Maddox demanded from somewhere as Fin dragged the fur around me and tucked me against his hard naked body. I kept feeding, content to be right where I was.

"Because I pushed her," Rogue admitted. "And she pushed back."

Damn right I did.

"Shh," Fin whispered again as his mind tumbled over mine. "We have you."

Fine, I'd sleep.

But he better not get used to this.

He smoothed a hand over my ass. "What if I want to?"

I'd think about it.

"That's all we're asking." A shudder passed from him to me as I took another hard pull. Liar. They were asking for more, but I wanted more, too. How much would I drink before this aching need would be gone?

"We'll figure it out," Fin assured me. When the darkness stretched up to tug me in this time, I didn't bother to fight it, just lapped at the cut as I withdrew my teeth and drifted at the edge of sleep with my senses full of all three of them.

Something was missing though.

But I couldn't quite put my finger on it.

A hot hand stroked my spine, even as Fin caressed my ass. Interest spiked through the drunken laziness.

"Sleep," Maddox ordered in a rough voice. Movement in the bed, and then he was pressed against me. Another move, and Rogue's scent filled my nostrils and he pressed an almost chaste kiss to my bloodstained lips.

"She is dangerous," he murmured, but I couldn't hold onto the words.

"But she's *ours*," Maddox argued.

"Yes," Fin said without reservation.

"This is a terrible idea," Rogue muttered.

Yeah well, fuck you, too.

Fin chuckled.

I'd have to figure it out later.

Then sleep swallowed me whole.

CHAPTER 9

"She's got the eyes of innocence; the face of an angel. A personality of a dreamer and a smile that hides more pain than you can ever imagine." - Unknown

The hard body beneath mine shifted enough that the arm tossed over me slid down until the dead weight rested on my bladder. Nothing said fuck off to sleep faster than needing to pee. Well, that or the gagging sound a cat made right before it coughed up a hairball.

I peeled one eye open. The shadowy darkness had a couple streaks of sunlight piercing it. The dust floating in those streams made me think of fairies. A fanciful notion because fairies were annoying little pricks and should be swatted with the same efficiency used to clear mosquitoes.

Shafts of sunlight.

At least, I was pretty sure it was sunlight. I hadn't seen anything close to it in far too long. The body beneath me shifted again, and I glanced to my left. Maddox lay on his stomach, one arm flung across me and the other under a pillow. The air might be cool, but the fur left his bare back exposed. Not that he seemed remotely cold. The bed was very warm.

To my right, Rogue sprawled on his back, his expression utterly devoid of any expression and out cold. Only the faintest rise and fall of his chest betrayed he was alive.

That meant Fin had to be my mattress and the owner of the stiff cock wedged against my ass. Fair enough. Maddox dragged his arm up my body, the weight of his elbow digging against my bladder again before he cupped a breast.

Typical.

I needed to piss, and I needed to stretch. Everything hurt. My mouth tasted like ass.

Considering I'd fed on two of them—all three if you included the feasting Rogue gave me when he first dragged me here—that actually fit. Removing Maddox's hand was easier than sliding off Fin. He still had an arm around me, and every movement I made ground his cock more firmly against my ass.

The idea had potential. Later.

Right now, I had to take a piss. Focusing, I peeled his arm away and settled his hand on Rogue's thigh. I sat up as Maddox shifted to fling his arm out again. Narrowly avoiding the trap, I grinned over my shoulder at Maddox cuddling Fin. They were adorable.

With care, I extracted myself from the pile of vampire Jenga and shivered once I hit the cooler air of the room. The fire was down to ashes in the fireplace, and the room was wildly empty of anything definitive. The bed. A chest. A low bench sat near the fireplace. That was it, almost monk-like in its austerity.

Hell, there were still sconces in the walls. It was like an unsubtle upgrade on the prison. Fun.

I studied the shafts of light though. There were windows placed higher up, thin, angular ones. They had coverings over them, a part in the cover was what let the light through. I was tempted to slide my fingers into the light to see if I caught on fire.

Still, I'd wait for that particular trick until *after* I peed. If I planned to go out like a succubus flambé, I wasn't going to do it pissing myself.

That said, the bathroom wasn't immediately evident. The only visible doors led *out* of the room presumably, not that I got a tour the night before. I limped my way to the door. There wasn't even a dressing gown or something to throw on to ward off the chill. Fuck, I moved funny. I ached in all the best ways from my thighs to my breasts to my throat. I put a hand up to the raw mark on my neck, and it was rough under my fingers, closed but puffy. Like it hadn't wanted to heal all the way.

Turning, I glanced back at the bed. Monk-like in the decorating choices, but definitely not in the sheets. All three males slept, sprawled together, not quite cuddling, and yet adorable.

It was amazing what a lack of talking did for a guy. Although to be fair, Maddox had at least *attempted* to honor his agreement.

Yeah. I wasn't that fair.

He was a dragon. He could have attempted a lot harder.

Fin was either a witch or a druid. Druid more likely. What that meant Rogue was, I had no idea.

And fuck, I had to pee. I shifted my weight from foot to foot, I gripped the heavy circular handle and yanked the door open. Fuck, what had they built these things out of? Thankfully, it didn't creak like something out of a horror movie.

The brush of icy air from beyond the big ass door hit like a sledgehammer. Fuck, it would be more comfortable to try and take a piss in an ice storm. I stole a look back at the fur blanket on the bed. I was tempted to steal it.

But I wasn't an asshole.

Most days.

Clenching my teeth against chattering, I hobbled out and pulled the door closed to keep from freezing them to death. The hallway had one long shadowy crypt like feeling going on. The shudders wracking my spine had nothing to do with the cold. It was old here. Too old.

Ancient whispers drifted along the hallway.

Yeah, that wasn't creepy.

Arms folded over my breasts even if my nipples could probably cut diamonds they were so stiff, I tossed a mental coin. Pivoting left, I hurried along. The place had a bathing room. Maybe the toilets were there.

The heavy fucking doors were all through this section. Some gave with a good shove, others just held like they were made of iron. I found two more bedrooms, no bathrooms.

Okay. Think Fi.

I couldn't feel the bottoms of my feet anymore, which was probably good, hopefully my bladder would freeze before I peed. It was bad enough I was running around bare-ass naked covered in spunk and flecks of dried blood. At the thought of the dried come, I swore my pussy flexed.

"Enough of that," I informed myself. "You should be nursing a pulled muscle after all of that. Or three." It certainly felt like I was. Not that I was complaining. At the end of the hall, I pushed open the last door and nearly wept.

It wasn't quite the porcelain altar of the Ritz with a fancy French bidet, but it was a working toilet with a tile floor, and rough amenities. There was even a shower stall. I flushed the toilet once to make sure it worked.

Since my breath kept fogging, I was surprised the pipes

weren't frozen. The water swirled away, and I grimaced as I settled on the seat.

Nope. Fuck that.

Too cold. I squatted.

I don't care how unattractive it might look or how much my core complained. At least the prison had access to a toilet without walking through the wilderness of a keep to find it.

A keep in the wilderness.

A sudden longing for my house on the cliff with its floor to ceiling windows and ocean views flooded me. Southern California was so temperate. Getting cold there would take some serious effort.

Unlike this gothic monolithic nightmare.

A long sigh escaped me as I relieved myself. Seriously, it took me a while to pee. I would probably be dehydrated at this rate. It didn't matter, the relief was so profound, it was nearly orgasmic.

Eh.

Maybe not that good.

Still, it was damn nice.

Finished, I cleaned up and flushed again, then moved to the sink. What were the chances of hot water in here? As much as I ached, I'd rather go find that hedonistic bathing chamber I'd been in the day before.

I'd also like some damn privacy.

I debated finding my way back to the guys or striking out to explore. The rest of me was rapidly growing numb, too. How long did it take frostbite to kick in?

There was no mirror over the sink. Well, I didn't really care what I looked like at the moment. Probably better not to scare myself. I did, however, rinse out my mouth. No toothpaste or even a toothbrush—not that I would borrow one of their toothbrushes. Suck their dick? No problem. Use their toothbrush? Gag.

With a finger, I scrubbed at my teeth, then wet my mouth and spit a few times. Not great, but between the icy water and my finger, it helped.

Top of the list, toiletries.

Second item on that list, clothes preferably, including a fucking parka.

Where was this asinine place anyway?

Once in the hall, I stared back the way I came then cocked my head toward the stairs.

Vampires were supposed to have really sharp hearing, right?

So I focused.

Yeah.

I couldn't hear much more than the faint whistle of wind from somewhere and the sound of my own breathing. Yeah. Impressive I was not. The lack of emotion was also telling. Every living thing possessed some form of lust. A lust for life, a lust for food, sometimes a lust for their next breath. Even the most devout possessed a lust for something. Shockingly enough, a lust for charity and a lust to do good things could exist. Granted, it was like having a plain potato chip with zero flavor and no seasoning—it could fill the hole, but it lacked any real satisfaction.

Still, the only hints of it I could detect came from behind me.

The guys.

So…we were alone.

Fine by me.

I descended the steps to start my hunt. Baths and clothes. Maybe just clothes, and I could get the hell out of here and make my way back to where I belonged. Then I could hunt down Dimitri and shove a cactus up his ass. I had stilettos thicker than his dick. Maybe I would start with one of them and work my way up to the cactus.

The heavy stone walls threatened to close in on me as I made my way down the steps. The lack of natural or artificial light wasn't doing much for the mood. I half-expected to Dr. Frankenfurter to pop out and start singing in his teddy.

Lips curling at the mental image, I tried to cast Grumpilstilskin, Dick Face, or Astral-Boy in the role.

Astral-Boy for sure. He had that angelic look and the body I'd been sleeping on would definitely look fine in or out of a teddy.

I descended two full flights of stairs before I found another set of doors. These things were big enough that Maddox would be able to fit through them maybe.

Huh, maybe that was why the place was so tall and wide. They'd had a dragon hanging out, probably saved money on the repair bills. Dragon would be nice right about now, at least he was his own heat source.

The door opened into a huge hall. Three steps led down into a sunken floor area. Columns lined it, and there were even larger gated doors to my right. I'd bet all the non-existent money in my invisible clothes those went outside. Based on their height and construction, they had likely been built with Maddox in mind.

Joy.

Twisting, I glanced at the huge receiving hall. It was like something out of the Middle Ages—right down to the throne on a dais toward the end. There were a few seats around it, but the throne was definitely that. Maybe not ornate, but definitely elevated.

So which of them was the master of the keep?

My money was on Rogue. He had that arrogance to him. In fact, he kind of made Maddox look like a pussy cat.

A grumpy pussycat, sure, but still a kitty dragon.

The idea made me snicker despite the gloom of the place. The ancient whisper drifted against me like an errant breeze.

Another shiver worked its way through me. Yeah, I wanted the mansion on the cliffs over the beach, not the old-world keep in the assback of nowhere.

Back up for the baths, or maybe down?

Wait. This was the receiving hall. Most of the stuff on this level would likely be for public access. I glanced back at the stairs. Those pools had heated water coming from somewhere; old world construction would use cisterns and aqueducts.

Downstairs it was.

It took me another thirty minutes of hunting, but I found it by following the smell of dampness, and it was tucked on a lower level on the far side of another huge open space. This one wasn't as decorative, but I could almost hear the clang of steel and the rustle of leather. A training room?

That kind of made sense.

I couldn't feel anything anymore. Once I shoved the door open, warm moist air hit me like a slap to the face, and I sighed in absolute relief.

Shoving the door closed, I leaned against it. It was hardly a workout to walk all over the place, but I was bone-deep tired. I headed over to the first pool and slid into it. The hot water stung my icy flesh, and I hissed, teeth clenching as the shivering and teeth chattering hit me all over again. I needed to wash, but I couldn't get my fingers to cooperate.

"If you'd wanted a bath," Fin said idly. "You should have just asked me."

Hypothermia kept me from letting out a startled scream or jumping like one of those girls in a horror movie this place would make the great set for. However, I did spin and punch him square in the nose. The sudden motion sent pins and needles raking through my frozen limbs, but the numbness protected my hand when a couple of the bones crunched at the blow.

Fin winced and put a hand to his face, even if the blow barely rocked him. A real smile curved the corners of his mouth. "Maddox said you were a fighter."

"Fuck you."

"I won't say no." His grin grew more teasing, and I rolled my eyes as I sank into the water. Sobering, he shook his head, then shed a heavy robe before following me into the water. "Come here."

"Why?" Hostility rolled off the word, but it didn't slow Fin down. He grasped my arm and hauled me over to him.

"Because you're freezing, Beautiful. And I can help warm you up." He pulled me right to him, one arm around my waist and the other hooked around my shoulders.

The hot water swirled around me, but he was warmer still, and his hands were like brands where they rested against me. He sank us down to sit so my shoulders were under the water. My tangled hair was soaked from the mid-length down, but I didn't care.

"If you knew I was up and looking, why didn't you just tell me where the bathing room was?"

"I didn't know you were looking for it," Fin told me, then kissed my nose. "My apologies, Beautiful."

I stared at him. "You thought I was wandering around this frigid ass mausoleum naked for kicks?"

A grin flashed across his face. "I didn't know what you were doing, Beautiful, but since you didn't come back to bed, I thought I'd watch and see. I figured if you wanted us, you would have at least come and woken us up."

Yeah, that was too reasonable.

I scowled. "Spying is kind of creepy."

"If I were spying, I would agree with you. I think of it more as advanced protection detail. You get your privacy, and I get to look after your gorgeous ass." He cupped his hand against my ass. "Speaking of which…"

"I'm sore, you can wait."

He blinked at the rejection, but his smile only grew. "Good to know, we'll be sure to take better care of you. Rogue didn't mean to be so rough, you know. It's just been a while."

And I'd had him on a lust loop. "The rough was fine, he's very talented," I said with a shrug. "Just I'm definitely sore in a lot of places." I lifted a hand to finger the puffy bite at my neck. I didn't want their teeth at my throat, but Rogue had bitten into me while he fucked me stupid, and I hadn't said a damn thing.

"Why the hell did he drain me?"

Fin snapped his focus from my breasts back to me. No, I hadn't missed the way he'd zeroed in on them after my comment about liking it rough. Pretty boy here probably didn't know what really rough was like. I could show him—after I no longer felt like I was straddling a bowling ball.

What the hell was Rogue that he'd knotted up in me like that, too?

Did they all knot like that?

Studying me from beneath half-lowered lashes, Fin traced his fingers up to the spot and a shudder went through me as he circled the bite. "You fed off the warden."

"So?"

"So, shadow demons have powerful blood, don't get me wrong. The more of them you take in, the more access they have to you. You probably had a craving for him, he came to you often, then started stretching it out. Making you wait a little bit longer each time."

Eyes narrowed, I nodded. "I figured he just didn't think I needed as much. He definitely fed me well."

"I'd keep that last part to yourself where Maddox is concerned. He already wants to kill the guy. If he finds out he was marking you too, it could be bad."

I rolled my eyes. "Back to the draining part."

Fin sighed. "Rogue drained you because we all need to. We need to drain and feed you back up. Your transition was sloppily done, and then giving you nothing but a shadow demon to feed off of is a terrible idea. You're vulnerable. We'll make sure you're not."

"Uh huh, you know what I hear you saying?" Despite my irritation, I relaxed more and more as feeling surged through my limbs. The hot water melted away the chill. "We want to make sure the only ones marking you are us."

"Not denying it," Fin said easily. "We can feed both sides of you quite easily, but we need to balance you out. I should have gotten to you sooner, Beautiful. I missed you by mere hours."

No skin off my nose. "I'm not staying here."

"A discussion for another day," Fin told me, then pressed his lips just below that spot on my neck, and I would have rocked off his lap, but he gripped me tighter. "Not going to bite. You've made it clear you don't want us there." Another kiss. "Was that where Dimitri bit you?"

Fingers curling, I glared at him. "Don't dig around in my head."

"Can't help it if you projected those thoughts of vengeance so loudly, Beautiful. I have no problem helping you remove his spine one vertebrae at a time."

Oh. That was a provocative image.

"Or we could nail him to the floor," Fin continued kissing a path to my shoulder. "Nail guns are really neat. We could start with his penis and work our way out to all his extremities."

"Vicious," I approved. "I like it."

His lips curved against me, then he kissed my biceps and glanced up me. "Bloodthirst is very normal in a baby vamp."

"It's not his blood I crave."

"No, it's his suffering because he took something from you that wasn't his."

Precisely. "And he's a moron."

Which was almost worse than if he'd done it out of some evil nefarious purpose.

"Does that bother you more because of his choice, or because you fucked him?" Genuine curiosity lived in that question.

I shrugged. "Probably a little bit of both. I just needed to feed, and I figured it was an even exchange. The sex wasn't even that great." Hell, I hadn't even gotten off at first. No, I had come later. He had though.

Twice.

Asshole.

I'd also died later, too.

Good times.

"Oh, we'll definitely start with his dick then," Fin told me cheerfully. "Not pleasing you was his first mistake."

Okay, I laughed. That was funny.

Fin's eyes twinkled as he grinned. "Feel better?"

"A little bit."

"Good." He pulled my hand from the water and kissed my palm. "The soaking pool is much warmer."

"It was warmer when there were big ass bonfires lit in the hearths, too." Neither of which were burning right now.

"I can fix that if you like, Beautiful." The offer came with another kiss, this time to my fingers. "Would you like a fire?"

I studied him. "Are you trying to seduce me?"

"Is it working?" He raised his brows and then ruined the effect with a laugh.

"Not really." Though he didn't need to try that hard. He really was very pretty.

"Thank you." This time, he dropped the kiss on my lips. "But no, I'm not trying to seduce you. Not yet anyway." With care, he stood and then carried me through the water to the steps before climbing to the second pools. Even though we were in the chilly air for a moment, I barely felt it and steam rolled up from our skin.

Oh, I groaned as he waded us into the hotter pool. Tension I hadn't even realized I was carrying faded away.

He set me down against the carved spots in the stone that made for a perfect cradle, then knelt between my thighs before he kissed me again. This time, it wasn't just a peck, but a genuine, open-mouth, tongue flicking, toe curling, pussy-clenching kiss that had me fisting his hair. When he lifted his head, he licked his lips.

"I'll get the fires started, then I'll go fetch you a breakfast."

Real food.

My stomach growled and did a little flip-flop.

"I really can still eat regular food?" It was such an idiotic question. I didn't want to be a vampire. But all they'd given me at the prison were bags of blood that I wouldn't touch. No other food. I hadn't had anything except water in weeks.

"Yes, Beautiful," Fin promised me. "You can have anything you want. Tell me, and I'll make it happen."

I eyed him for a long moment. Things that sounded too good to be true often were. "What will it cost me?"

"Nothing," he said, frowning, his playful expression turning fierce. "I *want* to take care of you."

And I wanted to believe that...

If he heard that thought, he didn't comment on it.

"Tell me what I can bring you to make you smile." The quiet plea there touched me, even if I didn't want to admit it. That, and he really hadn't made a move to get me to ride his cock. Impressive, since most guys wanted in me within a few minutes of talking to me. But he and Maddox had both handled it well. Rogue had too, really, until I lashed out at him.

Worth it.

"Coffee," I told him honestly. "I'd kill for fresh coffee, a gallon, I like it with a little sugar and cream. Bacon. I haven't had bacon in weeks." My mouth watered at the thought of it. "Real British fry-up actually, the bacon, the eggs, the English muffin, some pork and beans, and sausages." My stomach growled vociferously, and Fin's smile grew. "And clothes, my clothes, something I can put on because it's so cold here."

Lips quirking, he said, "I will bring you back all that you have asked for, though I might work on a way to heat the place. I like watching you walk around naked. Your body is spectacular."

I snorted. "If I'm naked, then so is everyone else."

"Deal," Fin said with a wink. Then he vanished from the water. Vanished from the whole room. I pivoted to look around for him, but he wasn't there. Suddenly, fire boomed in one of the fireplaces, then the other. The roar of two miniature explosions made me laugh.

"Nice," I called out. "Very nice."

You're welcome, Beautiful. I'll be back soon. Relax and stay warm. I'd like that soreness to go away so I can show you just how much I'd like to please you.

Okay.

That was hot.

I heard that...

Dick.

Heard that, too.

I laughed.

Well, I'd give them this.

They weren't boring.

CHAPTER 10

"Seduce my mind and you can have my body. Find my soul and I'm yours forever." - Anonymous

*A*s promised, Fin wasn't gone long at all. Long enough, I tired of soaking in the water. I'd dropped back into the washing pool and actually washed my hair and cleaned up before returning to the soaking pool. Conveniently, Fin had left an oversized robe that reached my ankles and had sleeves that went past my hands, but it was warm and thick.

Wrapped up in it, I headed over to one of the benches in front of the huge fire. Granted, the stone wasn't the most comfortable piece of furniture—would it kill them to invest in something less Dark Ages? At this point, I'd take eighteenth or nineteenth century.

Still, I was finger combing my hair while basking in the heat when Fin returned with a ripple of air and a distinctive 'pop.' The scent of the coffee hit me first, and I was on him faster than a one-night stand at Mardi Gras. He chuckled as he surrendered the first large cup to my eager hands.

I took a deep breath, and I swore I orgasmed right there. It was like manna from heaven. Or at least something like that, not that I'd ever had manna. Yeah, that didn't work. Here, just picture waking up every day for weeks to shitty circumstances, and to top it off, you get no coffee. Now, the really sexy druid not only brought coffee, he brought bacon.

I was so sucking him off after all this.

The first sip hit my taste buds, and I moaned. Oh, it was the perfect dark blend. Strong enough to fuel the fantasies with just enough sugar and cream to tie you up in silken ropes so it could have its way with you.

"You really like coffee," Fin commented softly, and I cut my gaze to him on the next sip. His lips were wet like he'd been licking them, and I didn't bother to contain my next moan.

"You have no idea," I whispered after I swallowed the next mouthful. "Bacon?" My stomach had begun to growl and gurgle. It really hadn't in weeks; I thought it had given up on me ever eating real food again, like a lost cause. I know I had. But this...this was better than sex or escape. This was perfection.

"I brought you everything you asked for," he promised, and turned to the rolling table that looked so horribly out of place here.

"Did you steal that from a hotel?"

That would be hilarious. Go to a hotel, order room service, just bring the whole thing here.

Wait, if we could do that, why couldn't I just go to the hotel?

"Not quite," Fin retorted, dispelling my fanciful ideas. Reaching for one of the silver tray lids, he added, "For now, let's just—"

The doors to the hall slammed open with a crashing force, and I damn near spilled my coffee jerking around as a rush of icy air flooded what had actually finally started to warm up. Dressed in only a pair of jeans and barefoot, Maddox strode across to us.

His fierce expression seemed on the edge of barely restrained rage.

"Someone woke up on the wrong side of the bed," I muttered. "Rogue not a good cuddler, DF?"

He drew up short with a hitch in his step. "DF?"

"Dick face," Fin supplied for me in an oh so helpful tone. "I'm Astral-Boy. I think he'd prefer Mad-Dragon, Beautiful. But it's all the same to me."

Maddox glared at me, then at Fin. "Why the fuck did you drag her down here? We're supposed to be together, where we can all protect her."

"Yes, because that long walk from Rogue's bedroom to here is rife with pitfalls as we waded through the swamp of despair to reach the hall of gloom and finally the lava pits of Marwen."

The dry look and tone were perfect. Letting them hash it out, I took another drink of the decadent coffee and hummed happily. On the plate were all the foods I'd asked for. Maddox reached for one of my slices of bacon and then let out a harsh yell when I put a knife right through his hand.

"What the fuck?" He glared from me to where his hand was now impaled on the table, and Fin bit back a smile. A circle of crimson stained the white linen as his wound bled.

"Don't touch my bacon," I said without missing a beat. "I'm starving, and Fin got it for me, not you. I'm sucking you off for that later, by the way," I told Fin. Then focused on Maddox. In truth, I hadn't intended to put the knife all the way through his hand, but the blade had been there and I really was hungry.

Without comment, Maddox yanked the blade out of his hand and nodded curtly.

Wait.

That was it?

Just a nod?

"As I was saying, Beautiful, before we were so rudely interrupted by your Grumpilstiltskin."

I burst out laughing as Maddox favored both of us with a surly look. He really was a grumpilstiltskin. Poor baby. I popped a slice of bacon into my mouth, and the first salty crunch had me moaning all over again.

Gurgling stomach gnawing on my backbone, I scooted forward to snatch up another piece. Fin said something about the food and where he got it, but I barely heard anything. All of my focus lasered onto the food as I took bite after bite. I was torn between eating the bacon or using the muffin to mop up some of the egg yolk. The potatoes were perfectly crispy, and even when my stomach hurt from how much I'd eaten, I didn't slow until I'd cleared the plate and drained the coffee.

I groaned happily as I sprawled back on the bench. The fire, the hot bath, and now a fully tummy.

I could die happy.

"Fuck," Maddox exhaled.

"More or less," Fin murmured in agreement, and I slanted a look at the two boys I'd half-forgotten were there. Oops. "No need to apologize, Beautiful," Fin assured me. "That was practically a religious experience, watching you eat. And it's been a long time since I had one of those."

Maddox gripped his cock and adjusted it until it stretched down against one of his thighs. I trailed my gaze over the thickness appreciatively. Not that I wanted to do much with it at the moment, but he had a very nice piece of equipment. One should always admire these things.

Males liked it.

And so did I.

Fin chuckled. "You know, when I said I couldn't wait to put my real eyes on you because you were a delight, I had no idea how delightful you really are."

"Oh, she's wonderful." Maddox made it sound far more sarcastic, but I settled for flipping him off.

"You don't need to compliment me, Fin. I'm totally making good on my promise as soon as I can move. You deserve it after that feast." My eyes were half-closed, and I wanted to curl up like Maddox's kitten and go to sleep.

"I'm very patient," Fin promised me as he smoothed my hair away from my face. "I brought you some clothes, but I think you're ready to go back to bed."

"I don't want to move," I admitted. The fire felt really good.

Crouching down, Fin tilted my head until I was looking at him. "We can take care of that, but we need you to answer something for us right now."

"Ugh, no twenty questions, just a little nap, and then I'll suck you off so hard, you'll think you came three times."

The corners of his mouth curved. "I'm sure, but one of us needs to drain you, and after last night, I thought it would only be fair to let you decide which of us it would be."

Fuck.

"You were serious about that?"

"'Fraid so," Fin assured me. "It'll be easier on you now. You won't be so hungry, and there's more coffee," he offered, like a temptation. "After you're drained, we'll all feed you again."

I closed my eyes and dragged an arm up to cover them. "Can't it wait? You're totally spoiling my good mood."

"Kitten," Maddox growled. "He should have done it first thing this morning as soon as you were up and moving. We need to flush that demon out of you completely. He doesn't get to have even a piece of you." His grip on my ankle was hot and possessive.

Pretty much described the dragon in a nutshell. I shifted and slid my other foot toward him, and he caught it then lifted them so he could sit with my legs over his lap.

"You both seem so sure they can control me…"

"It happens," Fin told me. "We want to make sure it doesn't."

"You know that's why the prince of the city threw me in there, right?" I flicked a glance from Fin to Maddox and then back. "He tried to compel me, and it worked as well as a pair of Jimmy Choos at a square dance."

Fin frowned. "Not seeing that analogy, but shadow demons are different. And killing your sire is really no trouble at all."

"Definitely," Maddox said, stroking my leg. "He should have every bone in his body broken for abandoning you."

Well, the guy had been running for his life and probably to keep his dick attached. Not that I planned to let him get away with it. Still…

"So if we don't do this thing right away, what's the downside?"

"The shadow demon tries to track you," Fin suggested. "Or call you like he did at the prison."

I narrowed my eyes. A lot of that escape was still somewhat fuzzy, not that I wanted to admit that. "You tried to compel me, or at least muddled me enough to make me cooperative."

"I did," Fin admitted. "We were in something of a time crunch, Beautiful. I will happily let you argue all you want right now."

"I won't," Maddox stated, but he smiled as he continued

his lazy stroking of my leg. It was kind of nice, especially since my feet were all toasty tucked up to him.

"But we want you safe," Fin continued. "Your transition isn't complete."

"Wait…it's not?"

They both shook their heads.

"Baby vamps need a lot of blood in the beginning," Maddox said. "For us? Hybrids? We need even more. It can't just be any blood."

"No," Fin picked up the thread. "It needs to be powerful blood. Your disdain for those blood bags wasn't just personal taste. I guarantee you they probably smelled like the weakass shit they were."

Fin didn't smell weak, neither did Maddox.

Nor had Dorran for that matter.

And the less you think about him, the better. Fin's voice slid right through my mind. No less possessive than Maddox, despite the lighter tone. He was still crouched near me, so I stretched out a hand to run up his thigh. "Fine, Maddox can bite me after I take care of you."

Fair was fair. He had brought me coffee.

"As sinfully delicious as that offer is, Beautiful," Fin murmured before he kissed me. "You first." He loosened the tie of the robe, and I would have complained about the chillier air, but he ran his very warm fingers over my skin. "And I remember," he promised as he began to massage a breast. "You're sore."

I really was, but I had begun to care less and less, especially when Maddox began to kiss his way up my leg, leaving a trail of fire in his wake. Their lust, carefully banked all morning, swirled up to surface. The languid satisfaction sprawling through me gave way to a familiar tug of desire that began to coil in my center.

Fin caught one nipple between his thumb and forefinger,

and began to pinch and twist. Arching up at the contact, I dragged his head down for a kiss. The first sweep of his tongue against mine, and I moaned. All sense of being replete fled, and I just wanted.

The wanton need didn't match my hunger at all. I wasn't hungry. I didn't need to feed on their lust, I just wanted to roll in it. Maddox nudged my thighs apart, and his breath was hot as he traced his tongue along the seam of my labia.

Fuck. The hot flat edge of his tongue seemed to wrap around my clit once before sweeping downward, and I was instantly soaked. The soreness evaporated as my pussy clenched at emptiness. His growling moan vibrated right to my core, and I tried to push my hips up even as I fought to wrap my legs around him.

Asshole kept my legs spread and my hips pinned as he begun to fuck me with his tongue. Fin swallowed every sound escaping my throat as he nearly matched Maddox's pace with his tongue flicking against mine. Dragging my hands down his sides, I found the snap to his jeans and pulled it open, then tugged the zipper down.

Fin cursed against my mouth as I got my hand around him, and I nearly screamed as Maddox moved back to my clit and began to suck against it. I thought he was supposed to be draining me, not fucking me.

Not that I was complaining. The heat of his mouth was next level out of this world, and he had my thighs over his shoulders as he feasted on me. Every hard pull of his mouth ratcheted the tension higher, and I ripped away from Fin's kiss. He threw his head back, panting as I stroked him from tip to base and then back up. His cock was long, full, and the vein along the bottom throbbed.

The musk of his desire clung to my nostrils, and I twisted, angling away from Maddox, even as he added his fingers to the fucking and teased his thumb against my ass. Hips rolling, I met him thrust for thrust. Fin pressed a thumb against my lips, and I sucked on it.

He groaned again, then replaced it with his cock, the first brush of it against my lips had me sampling the drops of pre-cum. I opened wider, and he pushed past my lips, and I moaned. Maddox let out a hard breath and pulled his fingers out. His clothes rustled as they vanished, and he dragged me downward. We all moved, Fin staying with me as he gripped my hair and began to thrust into my mouth.

The heavy weight of him on my tongue and the dribbles of pre-cum were doing all kinds of things to my system. It was like a heavy ambrosia, and I just wanted more. Then Maddox was between my thighs again, a hand stroking down my abdomen.

"Is this all right, Kitten?" The roughness of his voice had me soaking more. Raw, hot, and needy. What the fuck were these vampires doing to me?

Another pinch of my nipple, the one Fin wasn't caressing, and Maddox's hot cock was right up at my entrance. What the fuck was he waiting for?

Oh… Fin's cock bumped against the back of my throat, and I swallowed against it, pulling him deeper as I dug my fingers into his thighs.

Maddox was waiting for me.

I wiggled and pushed down on Maddox's thick cock myself. The head was fatter and took more effort, but at the first breach, he thrust home and an orgasm rattled through me. Then they were both groaning.

All three of us really.

They fucked me back and forth between them. Fin's hand tightened in my hair as he began to thrust. Maddox's grip on my hip was equally bruising as he slammed into me and his balls slapped against my ass. I flexed and squeezed around him as he pulled orgasm after orgasm with his clever fingers against my clit.

He came first, his shout ricocheting off the ceiling as he pushed in, and then the hot jets of him filling me sent another moaning orgasm through my system. Fin came second, and I choked as I swallowed as much as I could as the aftershocks kept rattling through me. Maddox swelled inside of me as he came, and I swore my eyes rolled back in my head.

Fin barely pulled out when the first graze of Maddox's teeth stroked the curve of my breast, and then he struck. The first pierce a sting, a hot tear before riots of pleasure exploded through my system. Still impaled on his cock, the thickness leaving me so full I could barely breath, he began to suck.

It was like he pulled me out with every sensuous jerk of his mouth. The soft gulps echoed through me, and I swore I tightened up on him or he swelled more. The world faded as he kept drinking, and I found myself anticipating each swallow. When he slid his fingers down to caress my clit, I detonated again, and the world faded entirely.

I must have blacked out because I woke to my mouth latched onto Fin as I drank, and he was trying to ease me away, and Rogue was there.

I had no idea when he showed up, but the shallow gash on his throat pulled me like a siren song, and I closed my mouth over his icy hot blood and drank like a woman dying of thirst. Maddox's cock wasn't buried in me anymore, and I floated on a sea of sex and pheromones and holy fuck bacon and coffee.

What a day.

Fin's soft chuckle wrapped around me like a caress, and vaguely, it occurred to me it was his hand stroking my back.

Rogue had slid his hand down between my thighs, and greedy bitch that I was, I had no problem when he started finger fucking me. I might have made a mess of him, but I pumped my hips in time to the thrust of his fingers as I drank.

Pleasure washed over me, and the next time I roused, I was straddling Maddox's lap, my mouth against his throat as he rocked me while I fed. Nobody was in me, which was nice, just hands petting me.

I floated there.

A girl could get used to this.

"You'll have to drain her next," Rogue said.

"I know," Fin murmured. "She's struggling still."

"We'll get her through it," Maddox rumbled, and his voice vibrated right through me. Fuck I wanted to ride him again, and there was a chuckle as he gathered my hair. "She's already getting stronger."

When I began to writhe against him, a hand smoothed over my ass, and then he lifted me up. The cock thrusting into me wasn't his, but I could feel his tip brushing against my clit. Oh fuck, I wanted to see this, but my eyes were already closing as the cock pistoning into me settled me like a lullaby.

Lust and blood.

Life's nectar.

The next time I woke, I was back in the hot steamy bath, sprawled against Maddox's chest as the hot water soothed my aching muscles.

If I thought I'd pulled my pussy the day before? Well, I think they'd totally wrecked it today.

"You'll heal," Fin said with a near blissful smile on his face. He sat opposite us, and I reached a hand up to pet Maddox's cheek. He kissed my fingertips.

"I don't mind," I confessed. "Totally worth it."

"Not hating being a vampire so much now?" Maddox teased.

"Undecided, but the fucking is extraordinary." It was a compliment, they should accept it. Particularly because I'd wanted, and I hadn't been remotely hungry. Sex filled a biological imperative for me, it was a currency I exchanged for feeding on lust. Getting drunk on their lust could be addicting.

Wanting them without needing to feed?

That was dangerous. I tucked that errant thought away before it could escape.

"Where's Rogue?" I hadn't imagined that, he was here earlier, right? I swore I could taste him on my tongue still. I could taste all of them, individually distinctive and heady.

"He's doing some things," Fin said with an airy wave. "Just rest, Beautiful. After you've napped, you can look at the things I bought you."

Oh, clothes. Right.

"Hmm. We're spending a lot of time in the bath."

"Complaining?" Maddox asked as he nipped my ear. I could barely work up the energy to swat him.

"Nope. Just this frigid mausoleum has to have more than two interesting rooms." Granted, I really hadn't done much more in that bedroom than get gloriously laid and sleep. Could say the same thing about the bathing room for that matter.

"We've got to open it back up," Maddox rumbled. "It will take some time. Just indulge us for now. I promise, we won't let you get bored." He stroked his hand over my belly and up to cup a breast.

No, boredom would not be an issue. Desire stirred, even as he began to toy with my nipple. Seriously, what the hell? I covered his hand with mine and tugged it away.

"Sore, Kitten?" Laughter underscored his concern, and he

shifted his hands to resting on my thighs. The swirls of hot water were definitely helping, still…

"Yes," I said. While true, it wasn't totally true. I could quite happily straddle another one of their cocks. The fact I wanted to bugged the ever-loving shit out of me though. Fin studied me from half-closed eyes, but he didn't call me on my comment. So either I wasn't projecting, or he was letting me get away with my white lie.

The brush of Maddox's cock against my ass sent another curl of desire to stir through me, and I pushed off his lap. I half-expected him to drag me back, but he didn't. Instead, he draped his arms against the side as I moved to another seat.

They were both relaxed, comfortable with the fact they'd drained me for a second time and I'd fed off all three of them. More than comfortable, I was almost looking forward to Fin having his turn to feed on me.

And enough of that. I rose and climbed out of the water, ignoring the sting of cooler air against my thoroughly ravaged pussy. And yes, out of the water, it made sure to let me know it had been well-used and stretched.

The tingle of desire grew as I padded, dripping, over to the fire and reclaimed the heavy robe. Dragging it on, I stared at the flames. Getting comfortable here would be a mistake.

The table was still there, the food definitely absent, but a thermos sat in the middle, and when I popped it open, the scent of still hot coffee filled my nostrils. Oh, good.

I needed to wash the taste of them out. Playing along and letting them get relaxed while I worked out my next step made the most logical sense. They were powerful allies, but they showed every sign that they wanted to *keep* me, and I was no one's pet or prize.

Despite Fin's claims when he visited in my cell and Maddox's insistence on calling me Kitten, I refused to be *owned*. Even if the nickname had begun to grow on me. I'd known them what? Three days? Maybe four? I'd lost all track of time, first in the prison and now here. After taking a swallow of coffee, I looked up and around. There were no windows in this room.

That made sense, it was below ground.

Was it even still daytime out there?

How long had I actually been fucking them and getting fed on before they fed me?

Would the sun still be up?

"Beautiful," Fin said quietly. "What's going on in that head of yours?"

Not glancing over my shoulder, I focused on the fire. "Can't you tell?"

"At the moment?" Something different shifted in his voice. "No. But you're concentrating very hard."

Good. As fun as he was, I didn't want to fall for that charm. There was no place for it in my world. Once I got this sorted out, I had to go.

Long-term things just weren't my jam. A weird little seesaw tug pulled in my belly at the thought of leaving.

"I was just wondering if I could go see the sun…I haven't seen it in weeks."

Then I held my breath, not sure what I wanted the answer to be, but that disquieting sensation over leaving them? Yeah, that could fuck right off.

They weren't mine, and I wasn't theirs.

CHAPTER 11

"Deadly is the tongue that only curls and doesn't stab." -
Unknown

Rogue

*P*ulling open the heavy iron doors, Rogue let
himself inside before sealing the entrance behind
him. Fin and Maddox had the female in the bathing room. It
was warmest there for now. He often forgot about the
temperatures here, so after he'd let her feed on him and he'd
satisfied her demanding need to fuck her—and his own need
to do it for that matter—he'd left her in their hands while he
took care of getting the keep more habitable.

Fin would bring in furnishings and had already
summoned several pieces from his place on the isles. It was
enough to add to the bedroom. They were using his for now,
but he would pull the other pieces from storage, including
their own beds. No need to sleep in a pile once they
smoothed her transition through.

The faint taint of shadow demon lingered on her. The

beast had pounded himself into her cells. Hybrids scared most of the vampire lines. They traced their lineages by how close they were to the seven, the original seven. The closer the links to the seven sires who made all vampires, the more important they considered themselves.

Pompous jackasses, the lot of them.

Hybrids were myths as far as most of them were concerned. Rogue, Fin, Maddox, and Alfred had long since faded from the public. They kept to themselves, and those that decided to hunt myths were usually never seen again. Descending the long flight into the hold buried within the mountain, Rogue didn't need torches to light his way.

This whole cavern boasted hints of ice along the rocks lining the way. Mid-winter, the temperatures were sub-zero. Maddox hated it down here, but Fin didn't mind it so much, though neither ventured too deep anymore.

It had been more than a hundred years since Alfred went to sleep again after only being awake a year. The oldest of them all, he had grown weary of the world, the politics among the councils, and the foolishness of young vampires wanting to cut their teeth on other species.

Old pacts and alliances lay in half-forgotten tatters as younger generations jockeyed for position. Rogue could care less, but it was those same politics that landed the turned succubus in Nightmare Penitentiary and right into the hands of a shadow demon.

At the end of the long cavern, he ran his fingers around the edging of the door, removing the ice locking it closed before he pumped the handle and pulled the door open. Inside the shadowed chamber, he paused.

Nothing moved. The heart beating inside beat sluggishly. One beat for every few minutes. Legend said vampires slept in coffins. Stories to delight and horrify the masses. While they didn't actually sleep in a coffin, those who went to ground often buried themselves far away from civilization, to avoid the sights, the sounds, and the distractions that might wake them early.

Deep in the hold beneath the keep, they were as far from others as they could get. If Rogue tilted his head and focused, he could catch the three beating hearts above. Fiona's beat far faster than Maddox's or Fin's. It had been racing when he sank into her earlier while she fed on Maddox. Rogue's own body had thrummed with renewed vigor since draining her. The shadow taint wouldn't survive within him, just as it wouldn't in the others.

They were old enough in his case, magical enough in Fin's, and just pure stubborn in Maddox's, that it couldn't warp them as it would and had been in her. So far, she'd impressed Rogue with her willfulness and independence. He supposed she'd needed those traits to survive, as her kind were often dismissed as hedonists. It might make fitting her into their lives a challenge.

Fin put too much stock in old prophecies and tales told over many cups of ale. She might not even survive her transition in the long-run.

The reason hybrids were so rare was they often died, a victim to their own dual natures tearing each other apart.

Quieting his mind, he pulled from that darkened pathway and focused on the draped chamber ahead of him where Alfred slept.

"Fin believes she's here," he told him.

There was no response, not that he expected one. The heart pulsed once, then went quiet again.

"I am only telling you because she was in Nightmare," Rogue said quietly, aware his words would echo back to Alfred when he woke. "She may not survive her transition. We may not have gotten to her in time. If they come for her, we will lead them away. If we must flee the keep, they will never get in here, but you will find us in Fin's lands."

The chances they couldn't hold the keep were slim. They would likely have a much harder time holding on to her. Maddox and Fin might be lost in their lust for the red-haired, red-eyed vixen, but Rogue understood the need to assert authority flaring within her.

She would run.

Everyone ran.

Maddox had, though he may not remember it anymore.

As had Fin.

They'd actively sought to become hybrids.

Well, Maddox had. His had been a conscious choice. Fin's had been a matter of his survival.

Still—they all ran.

"We'll protect her," he said finally. "Rest well, brother."

With those words, he turned and left the room, sealing it behind him before he began the long walk back to the stairs and up.

He closed off the iron doors again, then returned to the baths. She'd been out again when he'd left them. Her words reached him just as he got to the doors.

"I was just wondering if I could go see the sun...I haven't seen it in weeks."

The sun didn't affect all vampires. The naturally born had some immunity, but the turned? They all tolerated to varying levels. It was the longing in her voice that tugged at Rogue. She'd fed on all three of them for a second and in some cases a third time. The blood in her was older now, hurrying the transition along.

Did the sun bother succubi in general? Unfortunately, he knew little about the species.

"Maybe not yet," Fin answered into the silence. "It's better if we take the next steps slowly."

"There are places we can go that you can see it," Maddox added, though neither sounded certain.

Rogue scowled at her slow sigh. Disappointment curved through the sound. They weren't giving her definitive answers. Fin had definitely hedged his in uncertainty while Maddox immediately sought a way to soothe her. She required neither coddling nor lies.

Fin didn't know the answer nor did Maddox. The only way to know was to go into the sun and find out what it did. Hauling the door open, Rogue strode inside. The hot humid air billowing in the room wrapped around him. While he preferred it cooler, the heat was also tolerable.

Fiona stood near one of the large hearths, backlit by the flames. Though damp, her rich, red hair seemed to glow as it curled at the ends. A large dressing gown dwarfed her figure, and even though she was backlit, there was no mistaking her crimson eyes for anything other than her transitioning state. They were brighter though.

That was at least a positive.

"Come with me, little *sváss*," he ordered.

"Woah," Fin said as he stood. "Rogue…"

Maddox was already sloshing out of the pool. If Rogue possessed more patience, he would have rolled his eyes. As it was, he met the rebellion in Fiona's gaze head on. "Unless you want to wait for them to decide what you can or can't do."

Predictable. She pursed her lips, shot a glance toward the others, then to him. Weighing. Measuring. Who was the greater threat?

Who could she get what she wanted out of?

Did she even know what she wanted?

Fiona took a step toward him as Maddox cleared the edge of the pool. Uncaring of their nudity, they were across the room to catch her, but not before Rogue swept her up and then he raced her away.

Their curses followed him.

He really didn't want to have the argument with them. As it was, the armful of soft curves cuddled up to them had already brought them more than her weight in trouble. The keep's layout was oblong, tucked against a mountainside and preeminently defensible. A barrier wall and proud gates along with natural obstacles made them difficult to approach overland.

Most of their enemies who would seek them out were not human, however, and those defenses were mostly for show.

The true defenses were soaked into the stones and grown in the cracks between when they'd built the fortress. Magic, power, and blood inlaid all of the spellwork. From the most complicated and delicate to the most basic and plain spells for discouragement, the keep warded them against those who didn't belong with a giant *fuck off* essentially that turned away all but the most determined.

Hence the message he'd left for Alfred. Fiona had already begun to corrupt his brothers, even as she aroused Rogue in a manner he'd *never* experienced before. Already, the craving for her had begun to wind its insidious grip through him. He could still resist the influence.

Maddox and Fin hadn't even tried.

Still, the keep also had two courtyards. The outer near the main walls and the inner, where Alfred had once cultivated a garden. It was to that one he took Fiona. When the keep was closed up, most of the exterior windows were sealed and shuttered. Eventually, they might concede to install the generator Fin wanted to add, but for now, torches and candles more than sufficed his need for any light.

Fiona scowled at him when he stopped before the garden doors.

"Fuck that's cold," she complained, and he glanced down to see her bare feet against the stone.

If the stone was cold, the garden would likely be even worse. It was still late winter in the mountains. Frigid, even when the sun was high.

With one hand braced to keep the doors closed, he reached down and removed one of his boots, then the other, and set them in front of her.

Carelessly pushing a lock of her hair behind an ear, Fiona glanced from him to the boots, then back. Rogue said nothing, he only waited.

It was her move.

Touching her tongue to her teeth, she put a hand on the door for balance, then picked up one far too delicate foot and shoved it into one boot. It dwarfed her, so she would be hard pressed to move in those.

Might make running a little more challenging for her.

Intrigued, he waited until she had the second boot on and shuffled a step. A snorting laugh escaped her. "You know what they say about men with big feet."

"No," he said plainly. "I don't. What do they say?"

Amusement flickered across her face as she tilted her head up. Intrigued, Rogue studied her, uncertain of what her next words might be.

"They have huge shoes," she murmured, almost daring him to dispute her.

"That's not what they say." But he wasn't going to ask her to tell him. She had to learn to trust one way or the other. For now, he gripped the handle of the door and yanked it open. Cold air rushed in, and he straightened at the rush of fresh coolness. Fiona tucked the robe tighter against her naked body and shuddered.

The sudden wash of wintry sunlight blinded him momentarily. The light itself didn't quite reach inside the door, though the radiance brightened the gloom so intensely, he almost found himself reconsidering the generator idea of Fin's. Maybe more light would make Fiona more comfortable. While she would run, perhaps they could delay it.

She started forward a step, and he gripped the doorframe, blocking her. "Be aware," he told her. "It may burn."

Suspicion roused in her narrow-eyed gaze. "May?"

"May."

"That's very non-specific."

"As are we all," he reminded her.

"Oh, so you're a hybrid, too?" A smirk flirted with her mouth. "Vampire and what?"

"Older." It wasn't the answer she wanted, and the perfect symmetry of her face coupled with the husky laughter as she shook her head teased him. There was just a hint of green circling her red irises. They had likely been the color of a forest in full spring. Green, rich, and verdant... The sound of his brothers approaching reached him. If he wanted to test the baby vamp's survival skills, now was the time to do it before her erstwhile and self-appointed protectors arrived.

Removing his hand, he straightened and then motioned for her to precede him. He was fast enough to snatch her back inside if she began to burn. Unlike the ridiculous films Fin took him to see, they did not fall to ash in seconds. Burning someone alive took considerably more effort.

Most of them could survive it, even if it wasn't pleasant. And only someone suicidal or an idiot stayed where they were on fire without trying to put it out.

Instead of rushing through the open door, she hesitated.

Smart.

His admiration climbed a notch.

"What's the catch?"

Leaning against the open door, he folded his arms. "You wanted to know if you could see the sun. There it is."

"But it may hurt."

Another nod.

"You don't know if it will burn me or not."

He shook his head.

"You're very not hyper-verbal."

"I say what I need to say. Your lips are going to turn blue, are you going out or not?"

The shivers had been subtle at first, but she fisted her hands and folded her arms, hiding them. The cold air pouring in was not doing her any favors. She'd end up back in the bathing room until they chased away the chill.

"Wait," Fin called.

"Too late," Rogue murmured. "Your keepers are here." It was an unkind jab, but instead of rushing out to flout the possessiveness of his assessment and acting predictably, she glanced from him to where Fin and Maddox had slowed only a few steps away. The pair had taken the time to find cloth-ing, though Maddox skipped any boots and Fin had found his coat.

"Kitten," Maddox said, almost placating. "We weren't trying to hide anything from you. But everyone reacts to sunlight differently. It may do nothing. It might burn. It might just be uncomfortable."

"But we don't know," Fin picked up the thread. "Throwing you out there without any idea is dangerous. You're still in transition, and some people should remember how precarious that is."

"I oversaw both of yours," Rogue told him without taking his gaze off of Fiona. "I think I'm well aware." They might want to patronize her, but they wouldn't with him.

"We know," Maddox growled. "You have to stop just taking her without waiting for us."

"Or what?" Genuinely curious, he slanted a look toward

him. Would Maddox truly challenge him over Fiona? That could almost be interesting.

"Stop running your heads together like bulls vying for her attention," Fin stated dryly. "This isn't about *us*." *And really, Rogue? You're baiting Maddox right now?*

Rogue didn't have to bait the dragon. The dragon had already begun to stake its claim, and it would fight for its territory whether the man or the vampire realized it yet.

Trouble.

She might not fit with them the way they so clearly wanted her to, and no matter how much she intrigued him, Rogue couldn't allow her to tear his brothers apart.

Still, she looked from them to the open door then back.

"Please, Kitten? If you get burned too badly..."

"I get burned," she said with an almost careless shrug. "The fact that I'm half-vampire or whatever it is I'm becoming is not set in stone."

No. She might yet die for real, and there would be nothing they could do to stop it. Her body either made the transition or it didn't. The fact that she'd survived this long was a positive sign, but caution was the better choice.

"Also, I want real clothes." She swept a hand down at herself. "I look like a reject from a redneck survivor convention."

Rogue had no idea what that was, but the disgust in her tone suggested it wasn't a good thing.

"You don't have to wear the boots," he offered, and she rolled her eyes. Then stepped outside. Rogue barely got his arm up in time to stop Maddox from snatching her back, but Fin vanished from inside to appear ahead of her near the thornier vines, cold and dark with winter's frost.

The lack of smoking was a good sign. Pushing Maddox back a step, Rogue slipped through the door to follow her. The snow on the ground crunched beneath his bare feet. She held up her hand toward the sun, though the light of it already highlighted the glorious streaks of red in her hair. It wasn't just one shade, but multiple hues of red.

If the garden's roses were in bloom, she'd stand out amongst them as even more startling in color.

A sigh escaped her, and she tilted her head back, face up and eyes closed. Maddox came to an abrupt stop, and a muscle began to tick in Fin's jaw. Rapture was the closest Rogue could come to describing her expression as the sun shone against her faintly golden-toned skin. Out in the light, he could see where she'd enjoyed sun the before, though her color had faded dramatically.

Dying and being hidden away in a prison would do that to a person. Still, she looked almost—happy.

More, her heart, which had been racing, began to slow as she took deeper and deeper breaths.

"It's so fucking cold, but I don't want to go back inside."

Maddox brushed past him and slid right up behind her. Wrapping his arms around her, he settled his chin against her head. She seemed to melt into him, and Rogue didn't comment on the curl of irritation working its way through his gut.

The dragon shed heat easily, and the faint blue around her lips receded to pink and plump again as she ran her tongue over it. "Okay, that's really nice."

"Glad I'm still around then, Kitten?" At his tease, she opened her eyes enough to roll them, and Fin snickered.

"She's happy to have all of us around, she just hasn't decided on it yet." Confidence had never been Fin's weakness. Though overconfidence could be a flaw.

Rogue said nothing, though she flicked a look at him.

She didn't burn.

That was good.

They stood there for another ten minutes, saying nothing as she soaked in the sunlight.

"The library," Rogue said abruptly. The sun hurt none of them, so they could open the shutters on that room. Like the bathing room, the library also boasted two large hearths. It could be warmed appropriately, and the windows on both sides allowed the most sunlight all day.

"I'll take care of it." Fin brushed his knuckles down her cheek. "Don't linger out here too long, Beautiful. You still have clothes to try on."

"Did you really bring me clothes?" she asked, looking at him almost sleepily.

"I did."

"Real clothes, or dress me up like a doll clothes?"

The smirk he wore was real, and Rogue rolled his eyes this time. She wasn't wrong. Fin had likely gotten her something easy to remove or very little at all. It wasn't like they wouldn't be fucking her regularly, so why block access? The fact that Rogue was already wondering how long it would be until she needed one of them inside of her again and calculating how often had nothing to do with it.

"You'll see," he said with an unrepentant grin. A bird's cry yanked Fin's attention upward and Maddox's. A murder of crows descended on the inner garden, some of them alighting on the thorny vines while others took to the walls, and still a pair circled around she and Maddox lazily.

None of them moved as the crows drifted closer, then away. Those flying landed and sent others up into the air.

"Take her inside," Rogue said, watching the crows.

"They're birds," she argued. "And we just got out here."

He was very well aware of what they were.

As Maddox started to usher her toward the door, a pair of the crows broke off and cut between them and Rogue, then circled back.

Alfred?

Rogue shook his head. It wasn't unusual for him to summon birds to be his eyes. But he hadn't roused when Rogue had gone downstairs. Others used crows and ravens, too.

"Inside, little *sváss*. You will see the sun again."

Her mutinous expression gave way as she started forward. He didn't assume that meant she trusted him, though when one of the crows dove at her hair, Maddox snapped a hand out and knocked the bird away. They wouldn't kill them, because it wasn't their fault someone used their eyes, but they also wouldn't let them touch her.

Rogue blocked the next one as Maddox got her inside, and then Rogue pulled the door closed, leaving he and Fin to face them.

The crows rose up as one cloud of black. There had to be a dozen, if not more. Then they circled overhead and through the garden once more before ascending to disappear.

"Just letting them go?" Fin asked, tracking their progress with his hands raised and likely a spell or three at the ready.

"We don't know who they are being used by. So for now, we keep her inside, and you should check the wards."

"They aren't meant to keep out animals."

"Let's change that for now." It may already be too late. "After you get the library open, prepare the house on the isle."

"You want to take her to Oileán na Carraige?" His tone didn't convey approval.

"No, but we need a fall back point."

Fin frowned. "You think they are coming for her." It wasn't a question.

"You've had her, would you let someone take her from you?" They'd ripped her from the shadow demon, and soon, very soon, they would have driven him out of her fully.

Expression growing cold and dangerous, Fin said, "No."

"Then expect they won't either. Defend against what you would do, and know that your enemies might do worse."

"She's ours, Rogue."

"That," he reminded his brother. "That remains to be seen. She has to survive first."

"You don't think I know that?"

Still scanning the skies, Rogue shrugged. "I think you and Maddox have decided she is the one, and if she doesn't survive, you may end up joining Alfred in sleep."

When his brother didn't deny it, Rogue nodded once.

"That is why I remain skeptical. One of us has to."

A shudder rippled through the air as though someone tossed a stone into a placid pool and disturbed it.

"That was…"

Rogue was already moving, pausing only long enough to secure the doors before he raced to the hold below the keep. The doors were still sealed, but even as he listened, the heartbeat below had increased its pace.

Do you still want me to go to the isle?

Fin stood a half-dozen steps away.

Rogue nodded. *It will take him time to awake fully.*

I'll hurry.

Then Fin was gone, and Rogue touched the doors. "Easy, brother," he said. "No one has taken her yet."

Still, the crows and now this?

They needed to know before Alfred woke fully.

With Fin preoccupied, Rogue made his way to the library and found Fiona standing in the center of it where two beams of sunlight crossed. Maddox already had most of the windows open and fires going in the hearths. She was still dressed in the oversized robes and Rogue's boots.

The expression of pleasure she still wore flashed through him. The dust was heavy in the room, and it would take some time to clean it up, but she didn't seem to notice them as she soaked in the light.

Fiona belonged in the light.

For her sake, he was glad she could tolerate the sun.

It would help settle her...they could hope anyway.

Though it also meant one less barrier to prevent her escape.

Well, they would just have to give her reasons to stay that outweighed the primal desire to flee.

Or chain her up.

What a sight she'd make for them.

The image threatened to stagger him, and Rogue scowled.

The last thing they needed was for him to fall prey to her, too.

One of them needed to keep his head.

CHAPTER 12

"A cage made of gold and silk is still a cage." - Unknown

The next few hours passed in relative peace. Fin left and returned with food. Maddox and Rogue opened the library, and I didn't want to leave the windows, even after the light waned from the setting sun. Torches and candles illuminated the room. They really were trapped in some other century.

I'd kill for a big screen television and a marathon of *Property Brothers*. Or maybe *Fixer Upper*. Anything. Even focusing on my house on the cliffs seemed too distant to achieve. While I consumed the saffron rice and curried chicken Fin had returned with, he'd gone down to fetch the bags of clothes he'd bought me.

The first two outfits barely qualified as clothes, unless I planned to be the main attraction as a stripper in Vegas, right down to the floss and feathers. The fact that Rogue rolled his eyes at the second outfit made me actually consider it for thirty seconds.

The third and fourth were moderately better, but both were dresses. Cute.

Not my thing.

I preferred clothes I could move in and wouldn't likely tangle around my legs. Also, call me quirky, but I also liked dressing myself. The whole 'guys put a woman in what they want to see her in' thing just squicked me out. I wasn't a possession or a prize. I dressed for exactly one person.

Me.

"No," I said again and again in between bites as he held them up. The way he deflated with each rejection almost made me feel bad for him. Almost. If we weren't in a dusty library that smelled of old books, woodsmoke, and age, I might have. But we were, and they had zero intention of letting me leave.

The minute I said something about going to pick out my own stuff, Fin told me to give him a list and he'd get it exact.

The fact that all three had been right on me when I went out into the sun earlier suggested I'd merely upgraded one prison for another. Color me not shocked.

Down to the last outfit, I studied it musingly. Not bad. Tight leather pants, a black camisole top, and a leather jacket to throw over the top.

"Sold," I told him. "For now, I'll wear that."

He looked so earnestly crestfallen that Maddox chuckled. "You've disappointed him. He truly thought you'd like the peasant dresses he bought."

"You mean the itty bitty 'look at my ass' dresses that would work for a striptease if I didn't want to have to take anything off?"

Rogue smirked and Fin scowled. "They weren't that bad."

"No," Rogue said blandly, lifting a mug of ale he'd been

drinking slowly while I ate my weight in curry. The food was amazing, the flavors intense and sharp on my tongue. "They were much worse. She's not a prostitute."

Maddox and Fin both wheeled on him, and I hid my own smile. "No," Maddox snarled. "She isn't, and those clothes didn't suggest otherwise. A lot of women wear them these days."

With a shrug, Rogue said, "She's not a lot of women, and clearly she doesn't think much of the outfits."

Fin opened his mouth to argue, then seemed to think better of it. Finally, he glanced at me.

"If you don't want me going to stores, do you get the internet in this backwater of time and space, or is that still a few centuries off?"

The corners of Fin's lips twitched. "Make me a list. I have your sizes." Or he could just go get my own things. "I would," he continued. "Get your own things, that is, but they were collected when you were sent to Nightmare Penitentiary. I have no idea where they are."

With the way my luck had been going? Probably burned.

Food finished, I rose and slid my feet out of Rogue's boots. The fact that I'd worn the ginormous things even after we'd retreated inside meant nothing. It was a bit like having clown feet. If clowns had sexy, large feet that matched their rather well-endowed physics. Hard to miss the latter anyway. The minute I started moving, I had their attention.

"Before I get dressed, is there going to be draining going on tonight?" I put a hand on my hip because I really wanted real clothes on, but I wasn't an idiot. If they started on me, I was gonna end up riding all of them again.

Hey, if you couldn't be honest with yourself, who could you be honest with? As it was, Fin studied me.

"It is my turn," he said softly.

"And you need it," Maddox added, but the flash of heat in his suddenly slitted eyes had nothing to do with me feeding.

For some reason, I expected both answers from them. Yes, they wanted to help. They'd made that *abundantly* clear. But they were both rather fond of my body, and they'd made no pretense of wanting their hands on me.

Not complaining. Just an observation.

The one still keeping his distance, at least at the moment, however, was the one I focused on.

"You need to rest. Tomorrow is soon enough."

You could almost taste the surprise in the room, and I nodded. Worked for me. Crossing over to the clothes Fin had stacked on another table, I dropped the robe without a second thought. The bite on my neck was still puffy and more than a little sore. The one on my breast had gone the same way as had the one on my thigh. Wherever they drained me from, it would seem, had grown inflamed in some way. The fact that Rogue had done it twice was also not lost on me.

The dead silence as I flipped through the clothes for underthings had me glancing over my shoulder. All three gazes were pinned on me. "Oh please. All three of you have gone down on me, and I know at least two of you were under me when another of you was in me. This is not a new sight."

I stepped into the panties and tugged them up. They were pure lace and blood red.

Subtle.

I didn't care, since leather pants over a bare pussy was gonna pinch and sweat. I'd pass. The lack of bra also didn't faze me. I didn't like the damn things anyway. I tugged the black camisole on, but when I reached for the leather pants, Fin pressed up behind me.

"Are you planning to sleep in them?" The question whispered against my ear sent a shudder skating over my skin. It didn't help that he'd slid an arm around me and rested his hand on the thin sliver of flesh between the edge of the camisole and my panties. "It's getting late, and you still need to rest."

The invitation rolled through me like spring storm. Leaning my head back against his shoulder, I cut my gaze upward to find him smiling at me. Maddox was rugged, tough, and now that I knew about his dragon, I could see it in how he moved and spoke. He was a creature used to control.

Rogue? I still had no idea what he was, but powerful didn't begin to describe. The elements didn't touch him. He'd walked out into the snow in the garden without flinching. He moved faster than I could perceive. His demeanor? Quiet, reserved, and far from the argumentative and playful natures of Maddox and Fin respectively. The tattoos scrawled over Rogue's biceps and shoulders meant something, but I didn't know what.

But Fin was just adorable. Sexy. Beautiful. It hadn't taken me long to figure out his gifts. Druid. There was something just utterly compelling about him.

Thank you.

"Bite me," I teased, and elbowed him. He brushed his nose against my cheek as he slid his hand along my torso.

"Do not bite her," Rogue ordered abruptly, and Fin made a little huffing noise.

"He's a killjoy."

"You know, I already figured that out for myself."

Maddox chuckled as I untangled myself from Fin's grip. He gave me a hint of a pout as I faced him. The fires burning on either end of the library had turned the room toasty. Still dusty, but definitely warmer. Or the fact that Maddox was a little bonfire all by himself helped, too.

The fact that desire had already begun to curl in my

stomach irked me. I wasn't *hungry* at all. In fact, I was full and replete. Oddly, the blissed out sensation from the prison was missing though. I was *comfortable*. Not that I probably couldn't snuggle up in one of their laps or even on a chair by myself and doze. Be better with one of them.

Shaking my head, I wrinkled my nose when Fin beckoned with a curl of his fingers as he dropped into one of the armchairs. The little poof of dust that went up when he did that though utterly ruined the effect.

Laughing, I shook my head. "I think I'll pass. Or we'll end up back in the bath."

"You say that like it's a bad thing," Fin teased, his grin growing. He twirled his fingers, and a little dust storm rose up around him as it collected the fluttering particles in a swirl of air and then whooshed over to the fire. "See? All better." He patted his lap.

"Subtle," Maddox growled as he prowled forward and dragged a bench over to me. Snagging my abandoned—well, Fin's anyway—robe, he held it up. "You want this Kitten or shall I keep you warm?"

Tempting.

Fuck.

Too tempting. The pair of them.

Not throwing his hat into the ring, however, was Rogue. He merely refilled his mug with more ale and poured a second one that he nudged toward me. "We should talk."

Fin groaned, and Maddox scowled.

Biting back another smile, I set the leather pants down. Apparently, they were fine with panties and a top, but I snagged the robe anyway because unlike these three beasts, the cold did bother me. Dragging it on, I didn't bother with tying it. Ale claimed, I settled on the top of the table where I'd eaten—alone, thank you very much—and crossed my legs.

"Talking would be good."

No, my body didn't want to talk. It protested with the same pout reflected on Fin's too pretty face and with the same force in Maddox's scowl.

Lifting the ale, I had a hard time containing another laugh. They did not like it when they didn't get their own way.

Awareness crept over me as I took a swallow. The sensation of being watched, but the guys weren't looking at me so much as exchanging long silent glances with each other. Well, probably not so silent. Fin could do his little mental hoowah and let them have a private conversation.

Downing another mouthful of the ale, I considered the drink. It was darker in shade, a rich copper without the metallic taste of blood. Toasty and almost nutty, there were hints of malt with a touch of caramel and nuances of fig. As I ran the ale over my tongue and sampled it, the different flavors grew more distinctive.

Like the saffron rice and curry earlier, the different textures and tastes fascinated me. Another deep mouthful, and I swirled it around my tongue. There was definitely raisin in it.

"Fiona!" Rogue's voice jerked me back to the present.

"I'm right here," I told him almost languidly. "You don't have to snap." Despite the harsh crack in his tone, it hadn't really bothered me. I'd rather just poke holes in his reserve. That man had let loose with me and then acted like it didn't affect him at all.

Game on.

"Were you paying attention to the discussion about hybrids last night?"

"Hmm...I don't know, was that before or after you fucked me again? Or was that this morning? It's all sort of running together."

Maddox rumbled, but when I raised my eyebrows at him, he shook his head quickly. What? A warning?

Be careful, Beautiful. Rogue is not Maddox or me. He doesn't play like that.

I snorted, then took another swallow of the ale. All of them played like that. Or had Fin already forgotten the fact that Rogue had gotten me off before they even made it back from the prison?

"Hybrids," Rogue said, as though my comment hadn't registered, "transition differently."

"Right, I have to feed enough to finish it, but we have to flush the shadow demon out of me." I shrugged. "You've all said, hence the draining and me feeding on all three of you."

"There will be four soon," Fin added, the earlier teasing vacating his voice. "When he's awake, we have to have you ready."

"Wait—there are four of you assholes?" I motioned to the three of them.

"Yes, Kitten. There are four of us. Alfred's been asleep for a long time. He hasn't fed in a long time. When he wakes, you'll likely feel his teeth first. He'll need to drain you."

"Well, whoopee. Glad I'm turning into a glorified blood bag slash sex doll for you folks. Let me guess, I'll need to warm his cock up for him, too? Get all the kink out."

Fin winced, then tugged at his ear. "It's not like that, Beautiful."

"Little *svάss*, have a care. They are besotted with you," Rogue warned. "I'm not."

I met his cool-eyed gaze and smirked. "Liar."

It'd be better if he didn't care. Maddox and Fin already tugged at me in ways that didn't make me comfortable. Their lust was glorious to feed on, and I already enjoyed their blood.

There was a thought I never believed I'd give voice to

internally much less externally. Still…if Rogue were my enemy, this would be so much easier.

"There are four of us, Alfred is waking," Rogue continued. "It can be a process. We're only telling you because once he is awake, he will come for you."

"Any minute now *The Twilight Zone* theme is going to start playing. That, or *Psycho*. Are you trying to terrify me, Rogue?" Also, what the hell kind of name was Rogue anyway?

Beautiful. Fin's mental voice strained, but Maddox chuckled. "You are so absolutely irreverent. I am not sure whether to kiss you or spank you."

"Who says you can't do both?" Still, even as the comment rolled off my tongue, I raised my eyebrows in challenge. I could do with more ale, but I drained what was left in my mug.

Maddox grinned. "Good to know you'd enjoy that."

"Succubus, Mad-Dragon. I pretty much enjoy everything if it packs a lust-filled punch." Not entirely true, but I had a part to play, and they were getting all sorts of attached. I had clothes, and I could go out in the sun. I'd already managed to wake before them once.

First thing tomorrow, I was the hell out of here.

The thought of leaving twisted something uncomfortably in my gut. Time to cut out that infection before it sank in too deep. I couldn't afford to get attached. Succubi were not made for long-term relationships. Speaking of which… "Anyway, your point was we need to clear the shadow demon out, Fin needs to drain me, then we can have another magnificent round robin of ride the cock while I feed off of each of you. But you want to wait until tomorrow morning?"

With my new plan in mind, that didn't work for me. The more I glutted, the more likely I could keep on the move.

Particularly since I needed to travel from the dark ages back to the real world.

"Crudely put," Fin said, his scolding very present in his voice. "But it's safer for you. We're hybrids, our blood will sustain you like no one else's will."

"Dorran's seemed to be working for me." Even stoned me out. "Didn't mind his dick too much either."

Yes, I was absolutely pushing, and the black look crossing Maddox's face said I'd definitely achieved aggravation. So what if I never wanted it until I was starving? That wasn't the point. I needed them to let go.

"Little *sváss*, I warned you," Rogue stated. "Maybe we should just press ahead tonight. Eradicate the shadow demon's influence. You seem healthy enough."

A muscle ticked in Maddox's jaw.

"Oh please," I continued, baiting the hook. Or in this case, baiting the dragon, the druid, and whatever the fuck Rogue was. "I was hardly a virgin when I got here. A fact of which you should be grateful. You two knotting up and getting stuck inside of a girl could freak a normal person out. You're all lucky that I'm very not normal."

Fin chuckled. "And you very much want us angry, Beautiful. Despite what he says, Rogue isn't going to hurt you. None of us are."

Maddox surged to his feet, irritation vibrating off of him in waves. "Or is the point to push us away, to make us act rashly?"

I shrugged. "None of this is my plan. I was happily whiling away my time in a cell when you showed up."

"We will move this to the bedroom, save us the trouble of having to carry you when you collapse," Rogue stated. "Clean up in here, Maddox." The dragon was a foot from me, his eyes incandescent when Rogue stopped him in a single order.

"Fin, take her and feed on her until she's silent. We could all use the peace."

"Yeah, fuck you, too." Asshole.

"Oh, you will, little *sváss*." Rogue was suddenly right there, in my space, his mouth mere centimeters from mine. "You will be begging for it as you have each time." With one finger, he stroked my cheek.

"I don't beg." Ever.

His soft chuckle raked over me like a bad rash. Then he bit my lower lip. Not a loving kiss or teasing nip, but full on bite, and it fucking hurt. When I would have jerked away, he locked my head in place, his hand at my nape, and he bit down and then sucked at the blood welling up.

Not an ounce of pleasure stroked through me, nor was his lust even a stir. This was punishment, pure and simple. Pain for being a pain.

He was definitely an asshole. When he released me, the flood of copper in my mouth had me swallowing convulsively. He ran his tongue over his own lips, now stained with my blood.

"You taste better with each sip," Rogue said. "If only you didn't still taste of him. That is what we will remove."

There was just enough distaste curdling his words that fury roused in me. "You don't like it, fuck off. No one asked you."

Instead of responding, he turned away and moved. The speed of his departure took me a moment to process, but one moment, he was in front of me, and next, he was at the fire—with all my newly acquired clothing. From the irritating floss to the semi-decent leather pants, he had everything but the camisole, panties, and robe I was wearing.

He threw them all into the flames.

"You son of a bi—" The word broke off as Fin hoisted me and stepped. My stomach plummeted as the world wrenched around me, and we went from the warm, if dusty library with its roaring fires, to the cold bedroom. I landed on my back on the bed, and a fire burst into being in the hearth.

Shoving upward, I halted as Fin pivoted to face me, his expression dark and severe.

"Stop it, Fiona," he said, his tone unforgiving and without the teasing lilt of every earlier interaction. "You are trying to make us fight you."

Considering I could still taste blood in my mouth, I'd say I'd done a damn good job of it. "Or what?" Because I was tired of these assholes hauling me around like I was their fucking toy or fuck toy. Whatever.

"Or you will make this situation far more difficult than it needs to be for you. For us."

"Well, the gods forbid I make this situation difficult for you. Really wouldn't want that…"

Fin sighed, face turned heavenward. "I love your mouth," he said abruptly. "I love the way you smile. I love how it felt on my cock."

Shocker.

Not.

"I also love the sass you spill so swiftly and without mercy." He faced me then. "You're perfect."

I snorted. "Hardly."

"No, you're perfect." He took a step toward the bed and then slid onto the end of it. "I need you to listen to me, Fi—do you mind if I call you Fi?"

It was the first time any of them actually asked me if I minded one part of this whole thing. "It's fine," I said. "Only Elias calls me Fi, but I don't mind it so much."

"And Elias would be?"

"A friend." A real one. Did he think I was dead? I hoped not. We'd been close for a long time, he would be pissed enough that I'd fucked a vampire much less turned into one.

But that was a problem for *another* day.

"Interesting." He actually sounded like he meant that. "But will you listen to me, Fi?"

"I've been listening, Fin."

His smile was sudden and bright. Yeah, yeah, I used his name. Whatever. He'd been polite to me, why not show a little of the same back to him?

"Yes, you have, but have you heard us?"

"Pretty much. Also rather getting that you all think you get to make these decisions for me. The arrogance is rather off-putting. The magnificent sex does help in that department, but not so much I just forget you're all assholes who stole me from one prison to lock me into another."

Sighing, he nodded. "That's not an unfair assessment."

"Thank you."

"You're welcome." Another small smile. "Fiona, the world as you know it has changed."

No shit, Sherlock. Though I kept that last bit to myself and waited. If this was another 'oh, I was a hybrid and special, la-dee-dah,' I might cut myself just to get on to the feeding and fucking portion of the evening.

My pussy ached at the very thought, but damn if she wasn't already wet thinking about it. They seemed to enjoy wrecking me almost as much as I was enjoying being wrecked.

Like I'd said a few times now, I was definitely twisted.

"You're more than just a hybrid."

I snorted, but at his frown, I raised my hands in surrender and then flopped back against the bed. If I was going to listen to this epistle, I might as well be comfortable.

"I saw you in a vision," Fin continued. "Several centuries ago."

I rolled my eyes.

"You were the most beautiful female I had ever seen, one I

knew was perfect for us. *All* of us. You would fit with us and be our fifth. You would also be a hybrid."

"Well yay you?"

Fin levered himself over me, and I met his gaze.

"Fi, I'm not making this up. I've waited hundreds of years for you. Maddox has, too. Rogue…Rogue will come around. He's more cautious, but he's welcomed you here, and he wants you here."

I studied him. He really was serious.

"You belong to us," he continued, and I clamped my teeth together. I didn't belong to anyone. "When Alfred wakes up…you'll see. The balance is shaky right now. Without Alfred, Rogue feels like he has to look after us, and he and Maddox both think I'm too impetuous."

Well, I couldn't fault that assessment.

He cupped my face, and against my better judgment, I leaned into the contact. "I get that this is a lot. You didn't ask for any of this."

No, I really hadn't.

"But we can make you happy." Then he nuzzled a kiss to the corner of my mouth before laving his tongue against the cut on my lower lip left by Rogue's teeth. It was a soothing gesture, healing the bite. Too sweet. I swallowed. "You don't have to trust us yet, even if you kind of are. You don't have to believe everything, though I wish you would…"

Fuck. Me. "Then what are you asking me for?" Dammit. Pretty boys were like my kryptonite. Especially when they were sweet and wore their hearts on their sleeves.

"Time," he whispered, and then he kissed his way down to my chest, not hesitating or pausing near my throat. When he nudged the robe wider and the camisole up, I sighed. The heat of his mouth on one nipple fanned the flames of languid heat. "Can you give us time?"

When he sank his teeth into my breast, I closed my eyes

and arched. The first hot pull had my brand new panties soaking, and I cried out when he slid his hand beneath the band.

Time, Fi. Just give us time.

Dammit.

I couldn't see him, but his mental smile burst through me, and then he thrust two fingers inside as he began to rub the heel of his hand to my clit. The draining, the finger-fucking, and the smile—a devastating combo.

"A little while," I gasped. I'd give them a little while. Everything else faded as he kept feeding and sent me tumbling toward my first orgasm of the evening.

But it would certainly not be the last.

Not that I was even a little bit hungry.

This was all just for me.

Dammit.

I was so fucked.

Literally and figuratively.

CHAPTER 13

"More is planted in the garden than flowers and food. Hope. Freedom. Joy. They need to be tended, too." - Unknown

Some sixty hours after telling Fin I'd give them some time, I found myself chewing on the jerky of regret. I'd woken in the same pile of limbs we'd slept in since my first night. This morning, I'd been sleeping on Rogue, straddling his half-hard cock still half in me. Face pressed against his throat, I could still taste his blood in my mouth. That part hadn't really bothered me. Nor had the fact that Maddox had a territorial hand on my ass while he draped alongside me or that Fin held one of my hands to his chest.

I'd woken to sleeping on all of them. Despite how large the bed was, apparently I didn't get my own spot. Maddox seemed my usual mattress, but I probably gravitated to him out of heat. Fin though tended to fold around me when I slept on him, but Rogue and I were not friends no matter how good he felt.

No, the physical dimensions of playing human twister with all their naked limbs and their refreshing lack of any kind of concern where their bare skin encountered each other, these I enjoyed.

No, my problem was that morning, I hadn't wanted to move. Awake, aware, and intimately settled, I hadn't wanted the distance I needed to regain each day. I'd kissed the spot over Rogue's throat where I had been feeding. The skin wasn't puffy or swollen like their bites were on me. The fact that they hadn't healed had worried them.

None of them said as much, but I'd caught Fin studying those marks with an intensity that bordered on dangerous. And apparently, Fin draining me to near empty before I fed up on all of them wasn't the last time it happened. He did it again the following night, and the night before it had been Rogue who'd done it after he'd gone down on me.

The man had an extremely talented gift with his mouth, when he wasn't being stoic and distant.

The minute I realized I didn't want to move, I levered myself out of the bed and off of Rogue. His cock had already been stirring, as had a fresh pool of desire, and what the fuck was up with that I had no idea.

My panties and camisole hadn't survived that first night. I was back down to bare-assed naked and the robe I'd claimed. They always had clothes—assholes—and I hadn't figured out where they hid them. This morning though, I'd purloined the t-shirt Maddox had worn the day before. It draped me like a dress, and then I dragged the robe over it. At least I had slippers—a concession I was sure to the fact none of them liked my icy feet on them.

Well, none except Rogue. I don't think he even noticed them.

All we'd done was eat—Fin always left and returned with

the most decadent meals. He brought food from all over the world. So, my life could be tougher.

Sex. So much sex.

Even I don't think I'd ever had as much as I got from them. The fact that I was so full my body hummed constantly hadn't been lost on me. Then the biting and the draining, and none of them touched my neck. Not since that first night. Whether Fin told them why or not, I didn't know and I didn't ask.

Honestly, I didn't care as long as they stayed away from my throat. The fact that asshole's face popped to mind when their mouths brushed past on their way to what had to be their second favorite feeding area—my breasts—bugged me. The fact that he was still out there somewhere, alive and probably going about his normal life bugged me more.

I should have long-since gutted him. Leaving them to sleep, I made my way to the bathing room and made quick work of washing. While it was tempting to linger in the hot water, I needed time to think. The whole keep had begun to transform over the last couple of days.

It started in the bedroom—though I hadn't noticed when Fin stole away with me there. I hadn't until the next morning. In addition to the bed, there was a huge shaped sofa framing the large hearth. They'd added hangings to the wall, thick and colorful. Some depicted scenes of knights on horseback, others were of glades in the forest, another of the mountains, and one of the ocean with the skies turning crimson and orange as the sun set into the sea.

That one was for me. They said nothing, but it was the view I'd wanted from the bedroom of my house on the cliffs. Of course it was for me.

The chilly confines weren't so icy anymore. As I pulled the robe tight and slid my feet into the slippers, I wouldn't freeze as I made my way up to the library. I tried to go there most mornings. It was now dust free with more comfortable seating, and Fin had found an old style record player and a collection of records. The lack of actual electricity required we put batteries in the record player, but I was not bitching.

I missed the modern world. I kept half-expecting one of them to tell me not only had they stolen me from prison, they'd stolen me out of time. But I was too damn chicken to confirm that.

The idea that I'd never see a Starbuck's again or find out who Jeanette picked on *Match Me* was just too damn depressing. There were a couple of blankets in the library now, too. The side table was always stocked with something to eat. Usually breads and cheese. Sometimes meat. And as of today, apparently, jams. I had a sweet tooth that I hadn't been able to indulge, so I spread marmalade heavily on three pieces of bread, then worked my way through eating those while sipping water and staring out at the sun rising over the hills in the distance.

There was another oddity. Vampire or not? I was awake before the sun. Every day since I'd gotten to see it again, I didn't sleep past its rising. Whether I had in the prison or not, I had no idea. I'd been something of a morning person before, but not like this.

It also didn't seem to matter if I got hours of sleep or minutes. By the time I reached the library, the sun would be rising and I could stare out at the kiss of light as it flooded the world.

The marmalade tasted tart and sweet on my tongue. I should probably light the fires, but I wasn't that cold. My initial plan to leave had been shelved when Fin asked me to stay. To give them time. The longer I stayed though, the more I didn't *want* to leave. No matter what Fin believed, I couldn't just stay here.

Stay with them.

I sighed and leaned my head against the cool stone as I stared out the window.

A whoosh in the fireplaces told me someone was awake. The heat wrapping around me as strong arms slid around my waist told me it was Maddox.

"You should have lit the fires, Kitten," he rumbled. "I left them stacked for you."

"I wasn't that cold," I assured him. When he rubbed his bristly cheek to my temple, I closed my eyes and sank back against him.

"No?" Was that hope in his voice?

"No," I admitted. "Took a bath, came up here, got some food. Not really cold. Probably these fuzzy slippers that Fin found me." Fuzzy kitten slippers. No, I hadn't commented on them at the time. They were warm, that was all I cared about. Maddox chuckled, he liked them.

"Good." Satisfaction unfolded in his tone, and he slid a hand inside the robe. "You're wearing my shirt."

Yeah, I didn't ask how he knew whose shirt it was. "You didn't need it," I told him instead.

When he slid his fingers under the shirt, I laughed as he teased down to my thighs and then up. "I like you smelling like me." Then he nipped at my ear before stroking my hair to one side. It was still damp, but he hesitated when he bared my neck and I stilled. "May I kiss you here?" He stroked a single finger along the side of my neck. "I won't bite. I give you my word."

Something unfamiliar unfurled at the solemnity of his promise. Truth resonated in each word, and I bit my lip to keep from groaning. The hammer of my heart though, I couldn't control that.

"I promise, Kitten," he whispered, close but not actually brushing my neck with his lips. The little puffs of his breath tightened the coils in my belly. "I won't bite you. No one will ever bite you there again if you don't wish it." His voice darkened toward the end. "I'll kill anyone who tries."

The promise of death shouldn't turn me on so much, but fuck if it didn't. Tilting my head back to his shoulder I looked up to meet his gaze. The slitted eyes of his dragon stared back at me solemnly. He meant every single word.

A shudder rolled up my spine. I believed him.

Blowing out a breath, I eased forward. He loosened his hold but didn't remove the cage of his arms fully, and for that, I was grateful.

I didn't want him to move away. Shrugging out of the robe, I let it fall to pool at our feet. With one hand, I gathered my hair and pulled it all over one shoulder and then turned my head enough to bare that part of my neck.

"No teeth." The words came out trembling and without an ounce of the confidence I usually injected into my voice.

"No teeth," he assured me, and then pressed his lips to the base of my neck where it joined my shoulder. The pressure sent little shocks pulsing from my skin to my pussy and back up again. The gentle nudge of his leg sliding between mine had me adjusting my stance.

With care, he began to nuzzle kisses along my neck, inching higher with each one. The hum in my system began to ratchet higher. Maddox settled hit hands on my bare hips and pushed his shirt up. I had on nothing below it, and the fact that he ground against my ass sent liquid heat to dampen my thighs.

I reached behind me as he reached a pulse point and sucked gently, just his lips and mouth and the sensuous trace of his tongue. Terror and pleasure twinned as the erotic tease continued. He wore jeans, but they weren't zipped or buttoned. I slid a hand in to wrap around his cock easily. It was thick, pulsing, and hotter than the rest of him.

"Kitten," he whispered. "You feel good."

The barest scrape of his teeth to my earlobe, and then he went back to kissing along my throat. My head was all the way back now, baring it for him as he ran his hands up beneath my shirt to cup my breasts. The first pinch of his fingers to my nipples, and I couldn't hold back the groan anymore.

He thrust against my hand, but that wasn't what either of us wanted. I twisted in his hold, then pushed down against his jeans. Without a word, he released me and shoved them down to his feet before stepping free. Meeting his gaze, I hooked my hands to the hem of his shirt and pulled it off.

Bites littered my chest, and he dipped his eyes to trace each one with his gaze. Fuck, I could feel it as if he were touching me. When he cupped my chin and tilted my head up, I parted my lips, anticipating the kiss before he even claimed my mouth. I fisted his hair and wrapped myself around him. The heat of his whole body scorched me, and I wanted that fire.

The rough, cold stone at my back was a perfect counter-point to the hot, corded muscle pressing into me. He savaged my mouth, every stroke of his tongue had me arching. When he lifted me, I reached between us, and like we'd choreo-graphed it, I stroked him from base to tip, then teased his fat, mushroomed head against my labia until I'd lined him up.

Maddox broke the kiss, his gaze fixed on mine as he hovered there, just barely nudging inside of me. Licking the taste of him on my lips, I gathered every ounce of my courage and tipped my head back to bare my throat. He promised no teeth. His moan reverberated through me as he thrust in one, long relentless push. The girth stretched me as he pressed his lips to the most vulnerable spot, the puffy bite left by Rogue, and when he traced his tongue around the edges of it, I clenched down on him.

He held inside of me as I fluttered and squeezed, all the

while nuzzling my throat. System zinging from the contact, I ran my hands all over his shoulders and then into his hair. At the first touch of my nails to his scalp, he began to rock his hips. Then we writhed together, grinding and arching. He kissed my throat, my chin, my cheek, and then his mouth was on mine again as we moved.

This wasn't a frenzy or heat. It wasn't hunger or feeding. It was dancing. It was loving. It was terrifying. It was wonderful. He lifted my thigh higher and changed his angle, and then every thrust struck a spot inside of me that had me seeing sparks. I clung to him, the sweat adding to the friction as the stone scraped at my back and his chest rasped against my nipples. Then I spiraled, ambushed by an orgasm that detonated in my whole system.

His shout pleased me on a level so primitive, I didn't even understand it. He was swelling inside of me, knotting deep as he came, and then he had my mouth pressed to his throat. "Bite me," he pleaded, and it was a plea. I didn't make him beg. No one should. I needed to bite him, so I sank my teeth in, and he jerked as he came in hot shooting jets that lit me up inside.

We hung there, clinging together for what seemed like an eternity. Locked inside of me, Maddox groaned in between panting explosive breaths as I licked the wound I'd made closed. The mark was deep, deeper than any I'd left on him before. They'd all cut themselves to let me drink. Always opening themselves up for me to feed.

Not this time.

As I laved my tongue against it, I shuddered and clamped down around him again. I'd broken his skin myself. I'd bitten him, sharp and deep, and something unlocked within me that should never have been opened.

Beyond Maddox's shoulder, I met Fin's beatific gaze and warm smile before darting mine away, only to collide with

Rogue's icy blue eyes and satisfied nod. How fucking long had they been standing there?

The fact that I had Maddox balls deep and knotted inside of me still only made their fixation on me hotter. Maddox murmured something against my ear, and I closed my eyes. The depth of feeling when he said Kitten had me closing my eyes. They saw too much.

I wanted too much.

THE MORNING PASSED IN A BLISSFUL HAZE MUCH TO MY OWN disgust. Maddox didn't lord it over me that I'd let him kiss my throat or how we'd been knotted together for nearly an hour before he finally softened enough to slip free. He'd carried me down to the bath, and we'd drowsed there for another hour in the languid heat. By the time we returned to the library, Fin had fetched fresh food, including fruit, and I ended up napping in Maddox's lap like the kitten he'd labeled me.

By afternoon, Rogue had vanished and no one said where. Maddox had left me to sit in a chair by the fire without him as he went to deal with chores. The regret when he kissed me had been as tangible as the gentleness in his voice when he'd whispered against me earlier.

I still wouldn't acknowledge what he'd said. The words branding themselves deep inside of me, burrowing into places where they didn't belong. Fin came and went, all three of them busy with their tasks. Probably getting the keep ready for Alfred. Even as my thoughts turned to him, I scowled.

He would come for me when he woke. That was a cheery thought. Beyond those words of wisdom, they hadn't spoken about him at all. While there wasn't some digital clock ticking down somewhere, I could feel one. It seemed to flicker in my soul, an awareness that each passing second drew us closer to when the mysterious Alfred would awake.

I couldn't tell if they were excited by the prospect or worried. The amount of time they were spending on fixing the keep up suggested a little bit of both. The interior began to look more homey and less like a tomb. So I supposed that was an improvement. There was a set of windows in Rogue's bedroom—the room we'd been using—and Maddox promised he would get those opened today. That way, I didn't have to leave the bedroom to see the sunrise.

That wasn't the only reason I left the bedroom, but I didn't bother to correct him. Guilt wormed its way through me, like a cat scratching its way to the surface. Fin and Maddox had been amazing, and even if he wasn't exactly *warm*, Rogue had been a generous enough companion.

He certainly held nothing back in bed, even if he was far more reserved during waking hours.

Fuck, I was getting attached. It was bad enough they were attached. I couldn't get attached. Succubi didn't settle down, it never worked out. The need to feed coupled with how others responded to us…it was a recipe for disaster. Possessiveness. Fights. There were already rumbles between the three of them, and the enigmatic Alfred hadn't arrived.

What then?

Head resting against the chair, I stared at the fire. Music played on the record player—something bluesy and jazzy. It was nice. At least that suggested a more modern sensibility than some of the hand-inked tomes stored in the library. They had a lot of books. I'd looked for something to read that second day we'd been in here.

I gave up when most of them turned out to be written in Latin or Greek. Though Maddox swore that one was Aramaic.

Whatever. They weren't languages I knew.

Fin offered to read one of the Gaelic ones to me. Selfishly, I'd let him, and we were about halfway through the tale of the Fae who lost his way. Rogue rolled his eyes at the first few words of the book, but neither he nor Maddox left when Fin read to me.

I wanted to know what happened. That was another reason I put off leaving.

How much time was enough?

It had been a few days, and I hadn't been hungry in any fashion. They fed my body, my soul, and my mind. Too comfortable.

Sitting forward, I glared at the kitten slippers on my feet. I could still feel Maddox inside of me like was he buried to the hilt. Not that I had any trouble imagining Fin or Rogue in the same spot. I knew all of them, my body really knew them.

And I was getting warmer the longer I sat there, my body softening and growing damp.

Fuck, they weren't even present and I wanted them.

This was a problem.

Enough with the library and musing about their bodies. They were busy, and I needed something else to do. Sitting idle wasn't how I normally went through my days. Once upon a time, I'd actually had a job. I worked in a shop, I got to see people come and go. It hadn't been glamorous, but I enjoyed helping tourists find the perfect crystal and teasing real witches when they had to make nice with them.

It had been a good space to feed, too. There was always someone lusting after something in the Rising Phoenix. Always some young buck wanting the ingredients for a sex spell to enhance his performance or a silly twat on the hunt for a 'make him love me' potion. The first was possible to a point, the second was ridiculous. Bending someone's will to make them love you? Well, it *could* be done. If you didn't mind the homicidal rage it would trigger, the obsessive behavior, and the fact that the object of the spell would likely turn on you and murder you in your sleep to keep you with them forever.

Sure, no problem.

Nothing said love like a knife in the intestines.

Just saying…

Dragging the robe on, I headed for the doors. A walk to the garden maybe. It would let me get outside, and I could get some fresh air. I'd go to the interior one because if I found the front doors, I'd probably be tempted to keep running.

A pause rocked through me as I reached the gallery leading to the garden doors. Why not just go? It was what I wanted, right? It was what I'd been wanting since I woke up in the prison. I wanted out.

So why stay here? Maybe the shackles were sex and blood, but they were still shackles.

I glanced back toward the hall and the way I'd come. The scent of dust and disuse in the gallery was missing. There were more wall hangings up and wood piled into the large hearths ready to be lit. There was also a long table and chairs set up along the front of the room, and the shutters on the windows had been removed, though they were all frosted panes in different colors. The light coming in was muted, and yet still lovely.

Shaking my head at the inane thoughts, I gripped the door and yanked. It gave a hollow sound and a wrenching creak of noise when I pulled it open. Both comforted me, because until the moment it gave, I half-expected to find it as impossible to open as the cell door in the prison.

The rush of cool air brushed against my face. The sun was on the back half of the garden, not the front. The tangle of dark vines still had snow all over them, and the ground was thick with it. I hesitated. If I walked out there in my slippers, they'd get soaked.

That would be shame.

Making a face, I tugged them off and nudged them to the side. Bracing myself with a breath, I stepped out into the snow. It was cold, but not frigid. Maybe spring was coming soon to wherever the fuck we were. Still, I tied the robe a little tighter. The snow crunched under my feet as I tugged the door closed, not all the way, but to a crack.

Picking my way carefully passed the thorns and ducking below some, I found some patches of rock free of the snow and sitting right in the sun. Perfect.

Climbing up to sit on one, I turned my face upward. There was a distinct difference between the light coming through a window and feeling its actual caress on my skin.

It wasn't warm, and yet, it warmed me at the same time. My breath fogged in the air, but I closed my eyes, savoring the kiss of the sun and the fresh wash of frozen air. I sat there long enough that I should have been shivering, but I wasn't. More, I'd sat there long enough one of my keepers should have come looking.

But they left me alone.

Pleasure bloomed at the show of trust.

Or maybe they hadn't noticed my absence. Either way, it was nice to just have this time…

A bird called. Then another. Cracking an eyelid open, I shaded them as I squinted to scan the skies. A flock—yes, I know they're called a murder—of crows wound its way over the roof to fly through the garden. Weird. I hadn't seen them since my last trip outside. Not even when I looked out the windows the library.

Some alighted on vines, others soared back up to the rooftop. But they were all there.

And all of them were looking at me.

189

Hello Paranoia, your name just became Fiona.

Ignoring them, I closed my eyes again. I wasn't worried about birds.

The crunch of snow, however, sent apprehension shivering up my spine. One could be a fluke.

The second?

Eyes open, I twisted on the rock and faced the stranger standing in the center of the garden. Deep, dark eyes stared back at me from a bearded face shrouded by messy hair that hung to his shoulders. His skin was darker, almost tanned, like he'd been sun worshipping.

It was the absolute lack of expression that had my stomach bottoming out. That, and the very real sensation of power crackling the air—not a whiff of lust rolled off of him, yet he stared at me like he weighed and measured me.

Maybe for a coffin.

Licking my lips, I pushed off the rock to face him. "Take a picture," I told him with a hell of a lot more bravado than I was suddenly feeling. "It'll last longer."

Maddox growled and snarled, but he hadn't worried me. Nor did Fin, who made me laugh and could be irreverent and playful. Rogue, for all his reserve, infuriated me more than terrified me.

This guy?

The fact that I was half-naked and considerably isolated and lacking any kind of weapon hit me like an avalanche of bricks.

At my statement, however, the corners of his mouth tipped upward. It was the only change in his expression.

"Fiona," he said in a raspy voice. But it was more than just shaping his lips around my name, it was like he intoned all of me in those three simple syllables, and his gaze kept me pinned in spot like a butterfly on a board.

"Yep," I said, warier. "That's my name. Don't wear it out."

He cocked his head.

One moment, he was over there, the next, he was in front of me.

Right in front of me.

I hadn't blinked.

Holy.

Shit.

"Fiona," he said again, then tilted his head and struck. I had zero time to react. One moment, he was looking at me, and the next, he sank his teeth into my throat, directly over the spot where Dimitri had bitten me.

I was pretty sure I screamed.

Or maybe I just froze.

But the brand of his bite rocked all the way down to my soul, and then the world shifted as he began to drink.

Fuck.

Hello, Alfred. Some distant part of my brain offered the introduction as my life pumped out of me, and all I could do was cling to him.

Really not nice to meet you...

Asshole.

CHAPTER 14

"Clip her wings if you dare. She will grow new ones." - Unknown

Alfred

*T*he first whispers reached him when Fin came to see Rogue.

"She's there, I know it's her." Always optimistic and profound in his faith.

"You can't know it's her." Always the skeptic, warier and cautious.

"I do know," Fin insisted. "She's a succubus, or she was. Some idiot drained her while screwing her, and instead of letting her heal naturally, he panicked."

Rogue's sigh carried the weight of the ages. "He force fed her blood?"

"Far as I can tell. A lot of people don't want to talk about it. Their prince has ordered silence. I got there an hour after they took her. She went right for him—the prince and the asshole."

"Where's the asshole now?"

Yes, he would like to know this, too.

"In the wind." Frustration etched Fin's words. "I'll find him, or Maddox will. For now, we need to get to her. The prince sent her to Nightmare Penitentiary. He's determined to cover this up before the American council learns about her. Hybrids are myths after all."

A snort. "You want to go after her."

Then silence.

"Fin."

"Maddox is on his way in. It took me time to track an access point. They've improved their spellkeepers on the gates. Not that much, but he's on his way in. I'm going after him."

"And you're telling me because you want me to come…"

"Just back up. If you haven't heard from us…"

The words faded as they argued. Rogue would go. He wouldn't leave their brothers alone, not if they asked for him.

He drifted.

"Rogue…why the hell did you do that?" Maddox's snarl ripped through his sleep.

"Because she stinks of shadow demon, and if you hadn't noticed, he can already call her."

"I was blocking him," Fin argued.

"She's not even through transition." The disgust curling in Rogue's tone roused him further. "We'll need to drain her, repeatedly. Lance the shadow from her, break the addiction, then infuse her with our blood."

"That will save her?" Hope crept into Maddox's tone. A hope that hadn't been present in so long, Alfred had forgotten the last time he heard it. He was one of the last of his kind. Maybe the very last.

They'd saved him from the hunters who came for him. He and Rogue had both protected the wounded beast and found a friend.

A brother.

"There are no guarantees, Maddox," Rogue told him, and no one but Alfred would have heard the sympathy in his tone. "We'll try."

"What about Alfred?" Fin said. "We should wake him. She's the one."

"We don't know she is," Rogue reprimanded him. "Alfred will wake when he's ready."

Was he even truly asleep?

They seemed to have it in hand.

The slam of a rapid heart and screams of ecstasy ricocheted off the walls. A scent tickled at his nostrils.

"…you're not wrong," Fin agreed. "But I can be jealous because I want to know her, too. I've dreamt about her for centuries. Unlike the rest of you, I knew she was coming. I never broke faith."

"Lust-filled dreams about her breasts are not what I would call prophetic," Maddox stated drily, and Rogue gave a half-laugh.

He dozed.

"Ask me no questions, and I'll tell you no lies." Her husky voice wrapped around him like a lure.

Maddox snarled, "Stop poking in her head. We're supposed to be convincing her, not chasing her away."

"I was playing," Fin argued. "Besides, she thinks I'm pretty. So suck it."

Flashes of impatience from Rogue. The boys argued. They always had. It was good for them. It kept them alive.

"…what the fuck were you thinking?"

"He's lust drunk, what do you think he was thinking?" Fin snapped. "Just feed her. He's all knotted up inside her and not moving for a while."

Quiet again.

Movement roused him. Movement and pain. He tried to

focus on it. The stranger moving about the keep. Her light steps landed like warning thuds. Change eddied in the air. Change he hadn't tasted in generations.

It wasn't time yet.

"…shadow demon…"

Hmm. What was that about a shadow demon? Demons kept their distance. They knew better than to disturb him or his.

The thread faded away.

"…Fin believes she's here." Rogue. "I am only telling you because she was in Nightmare Penitentiary. She may not survive her transition. We may not have gotten to her in time. If they come for her, we will lead them away. If we must flee the keep, they will never get in here, but you will find us in Fin's lands."

If *they* come for her?

Someone hunted her?

His sleeping mind turned the information over.

Shadow demon.

Prison.

Yes. They might try to come for her.

No one invaded his lands.

"I was just wondering if I could go see the sun…I haven't seen it in weeks."

Her voice whispered to him, beckoning, and he listened to the shift in her heartbeat. To the discussion from the boys wanting her to not risk it. Vampires in transition were particularly vulnerable. If the transition wasn't taking, the sun was the fastest way to end their suffering.

Not all vampires could walk in the sun. The bloodlines had begun to weaken. The natural born retained some of the skill, but the turned? More and more, they faded too quickly. Power and hunger had made selection an open market rather than a chosen few carefully shepherded.

Selfish bastards.

Movement against his wards had him stirring.

Crows.

They swarmed toward his garden. Another power touched their minds, and he dislodged it easily. This was his keep. His land. Everything on it was his. The interloper fled at the first brush. An image scorched against his mind, a challenge.

Then he stared into the garden through the eyes of the many. Red hair snagged his attention, full lips and pale golden skin.

The red eyes pulled all his focus, and her pout when they insisted she return inside. He agreed, he didn't want her to go, but then she was gone, and Rogue stared at the crows with a warning on his face.

It had been a long time since he'd lain eyes on his brothers. Rogue didn't know it was him, he worried it was the other.

Then they were gone, and Alfred let his mind wander as the crows flew. Time had marched on. How much had passed, he wasn't certain. He needed to find out.

Anger.

Rebellion.

Lust.

The scent of it permeated the keep. Fiona.

Her name was Fiona.

Maddox called her Kitten.

Fin labeled her Beautiful.

But it was Rogue's nickname that pulled at him. Little *svāss*.

Little Beloved.

His heart rate began to increase. They were courting her. Draining her. Feeding her. Fin pled with her for more time. The little hellion wanted to leave. They always ran. But it had

197

been a few days, and she was still in the keep. She still fed from them, and her signature and scent grew stronger every day.

Alfred wanted to see her

Wanted to test her.

Taste her.

Awareness rippled through the keep as a door opened and she left. Her heartbeat grew more distant. He'd been listening to it for days now, the cadence of her heart. When it sped, when it slowed, when it pumped furiously as one of his brothers pleasured her. He understood each rhythm. It slowed and grew fainter as she left the safety of the interior for the sun.

The crows came at his summoning. At his first glimpse of the firebrand's hair, his pulse quickened. The chamber opened with a single wave of his hand, and he stepped out. Hunger assailed him.

Hunger and need.

Like a ghost, he moved through the keep. The locks fell away at his presence. The spells infused into the stone had also used his blood. Outside, the sun warmed his skin and blinded him, but he didn't need his own eyes. The crows gave him all the angles he needed. Her tousled curls. Her full lips. The fact that she wore only a robe and her feet were bare despite the snow.

The flush to her cheeks.

Life suffused the hellion. Life and power.

The first whiff of her stroked through him as he took a deep breath, filling his lungs with the musky femininity. All of his brothers had marked her. The breeze shifted her hair, baring the bite mark on her neck. The puffiness of it hadn't faded. The transition wasn't complete.

They'd kept her alive.

There, just below the sweetness of her perfume and the

overlays of his brothers blanketing her scent, was the taint of shadow. It was still there, like a dark invader lurking beneath her skin.

The demon had done more than just mark blood and her body. He'd marked her soul. It was as much a declaration of property as it was of war. Alfred met her gaze when she jerked to look at him.

Red eyes blazed back at him. But they hadn't always been red. No, that color belonged to his hellion's hair, not her eyes. She needed to complete the transition, to let go of the dual ties and sink into the place she belonged.

Fin might be right about her.

While he'd shared the vision, Alfred had never seen the woman's face. Only her hair.

The same scarlet hair now blowing in the wind. A wind that shifted and flooded him with her scent. Hers, theirs, and the shadow demon's.

Hunger assailed him.

She ran her tongue over her lips, trapping his attention on her luscious mouth. "Take a picture," she challenged as she pushed up from the rock to face him. "It'll last longer."

Amusement curved through him. Defiant.

No wonder his brothers couldn't get enough of her.

She had spirit.

"Fiona," he tested her name on his tongue. Everything about her seemed encapsulated in her name. Queen and demon. Lover and threat. Friend and enemy. Fiona was far more dangerous than she realized.

Dangerous.

Beautiful.

Intoxicating.

"Yep," she replied, brazen in her challenge. Not once did she dip her eyes. Most vampires couldn't meet his gaze head on. Most couldn't even look in his direction. Fiona? She raised that chin and straightened her spine. "That's my name. Don't wear it out."

Lust punched through him. Burrowing beneath his skin to arouse a hunger he hadn't experienced...*ever*.

He closed the distance. The need to touch her overrode everything.

"Fiona," he whispered the hellion's name with the reverence she deserved. The fact that the shadow demon's taint still stained her incensed him. No more. His brothers had tried to erase it. Alfred would remove it entirely. His eyes narrowed on the mark on her throat. Unlike the others, it had faded to a near scar. It was the first one. The one that would remain, even after the others cleared from transition.

It was the mark of the one who made her.

Quiet fury suddenly bubbled in his sluggish system, quickening the pace of his heart and flushing him from inaction to reaction. No one else was allowed to mark her. Not the shadow demon.

Not the bastard vampire.

The need to obliterate their marks and replace it with his own surged like electricity through his blood. He sank his teeth into that mark, his arms locked around her to keep her still. The last thing he wanted to do was tear out her throat. The soft vulnerable column was not a match for the pierce of his teeth as he sank into her sweet flesh.

The first dribble of her blood over his tongue, and he locked his lips to suck deeply. The hot liquid quenched his parched throat, sating both his desire and starving him for more. Every flash of hot decadence rolling around his tongue let him taste her. Her whole body softened against him, the sweet tang of her need adding to the spice on his tongue.

Hello, Alfred. Her biting words lashed at him, even as she gripped his shoulders, clinging to him though she was in no

danger of falling. He had her. *Really not nice to meet you...
Asshole.*

He plunged deeper, drawing it from her. All of it.

All of her.

*"You're new," the male said as he slid onto the stool next
to me. New? Really? What a tired line. I slanted a look at him
without turning. The mirror behind the bar gave me a good visual.*

*He was lean, dark-brown eyes and hair. He possessed a boyish
kind of charm, and his appearance was impeccable. His clothing
was upscale and expensive. He'd shaved recently, and his fingers
were long and slender. They reminded me of a musician's hands.
Beyond all of that, his lust was a potent force, shimmering off of
him in waves. All of it focused on me.*

*I'd been hungry for the last three days, and despite wandering
the various bars, I'd yet to find someone I could feast on that I
wouldn't hurt. My fault for waiting too long between feedings. I'd
been leaching a little here and there to stave off the overriding need.
But with full moon and the partying pagans gathering along with a
huge influx of supernatural over the last two weeks, I had to play it
safer.*

*Elias would have helped out, but we were friends, and fucking
friends was usually a no-no in my book. The very last friend I'd
fucked to feed on had grown obsessed, and our friendship died in
the ashes of his lust.*

*No, I kept my feeding separate from the rest of my life. Just so
much easier.*

*This guy...he wasn't human. If I had to guess, I'd say vampire.
He was almost too pretty to be anything else. Still...vampires were
usually no gos. They wanted more than fucking, and while they
could be amazing in bed, Elias had a real problem anytime I
indulged my more dangerous fantasies.*

Still, beggars couldn't be choosers, and I was so damn hungry.

"Hello," I answered, leaning in to let his lust lick over my skin. Oh, it was delicious, and his pupils dilated as he narrowed the distance even further. I wasn't the only one who was hungry.

Oh, this could work out.

One drink, and we were in a private booth and I had his cock halfway down my throat as he thrust up, desperate for the release as I stroked his balls. The feverish grip of his fingers in my hair pushed me to take him deeper, even as his lust swelled like his cock. When he came, it was a burst of salty bitterness and sweet satisfaction. The wildness of it swarmed through me with a punch more potent than the liquor he'd ordered for me.

His whole body shuddered as he dragged me up, and then his mouth was on mine. The fact that I could still taste his spunk—which meant he could too—amused me on some level, but it didn't deter him in the slightest. If anything, it amplified his need.

When he shredded my panties and I climbed on him in the booth, it was a quick and furious coupling magnified by the beat of music around us. I loved the outfit, the leather dress and the sexy heels. The leather massaged my nipples as I moved, the buttery softness a fantastic counterpoint to the hardness of the cock he slammed me down on.

The guy's technique was lacking, but fuck if he didn't make up for it with enthusiasm. He bit my wrist after the second set of orgasms. His, not mine. He didn't last long enough for mine, but I wasn't here to get off so much as to just feed, and yeah, I was more than a little drunk on him.

The lust rolling off him grew more potent rather than diminishing. When he bit down on my wrist and fingered my clit until I came, I blissed out. Probably explained why I left with him, his come still sticky on my thighs, and why I let him take me back to his place.

Well that, and I wasn't inviting him to my shitty little apartment. It might be small and cramped, but it was mine. I was saving *everything to build my perfect place. I could see where I wanted it and how I wanted it to be. I was always redesigning it.*

His place was much nicer and a penthouse.

Yeah, this dude was loaded.

We were three steps in the door when he was on me again, and fuck if I didn't just go down for all that fierce snarling. He slammed me against a wall—yeah, it was kind of hot, and he had the dress pushed up as he fucked into me. When he bit my neck, I didn't think anything about it.

Fair was fair. I was drowning in his lust, and he was getting off. But a guy had to eat. I'd just wait until the bite marks healed before seeing Elias.

Even after he came again, I was still feeling it. Fuck, it would be nice to be able to feed and get off at the same time. Pants open, he carried me into his room. It was so fucking over the top melodramatic, I started laughing.

Literally, black silk sheets, black wall hangings, black walls—if he'd had a coffin shaped bed, it would have fit right in with the aesthetic.

"What the fuck are you laughing at?" he demanded as he dumped me on the bed.

"Aww, poor baby, did I hurt you feelings?" Okay, so I was a little drunk, pointing one of my heeled feet at him and mocking him just a little. It was no reason to rip the shoe off and snap the heel.

Those were my best pair of shoes.

"I think you have too much energy," he growled. "You need to remember who you're here to serve."

Really?

I slugged him.

It broke my hand, but whatever. When he ripped the dress open though, oh it was on. The problem was that I was already lust drunk, and the more I fought, the more it fanned his lust. Fuck, I didn't care how rough he made it. Or that he half strangled me when he mounted me. The moment his teeth sank into my throat, I was groaning. I came over and over, but more from the lust pounding into me than his body.

Then the world darkened as he wouldn't let go, and the pain pierced the pleasure. I fought to get his teeth out of me, but all he did was moan and suck harder, his hips pistoning until the world blotted out.

Then I was choking on blood. So much blood. It was pouring down my throat until I gagged.

I didn't want it.

Didn't he understand...

Terror clawed at me when I woke.

Blood coated my mouth.

The room was wrecked.

My clothes shredded.

Dimitri was gone. No sign of him anywhere.

I staggered into the bathroom and stared at the red eyes staring back at me.

What the fuck had he done?

Terror turned to rage.

I was going to kill me a vampire.

He'd wrecked my favorite outfit. Broken my favorite pair of shoes. Beyond all that, he'd poured his blood down my throat.

I couldn't be a vampire, but my noodle like limbs and weakness decried all of that.

I didn't heal from blood.

I didn't...

ALFRED LIFTED HIS HEAD. SHE'D GONE UTTERLY LIMP IN HIS arms. Images kept flashing through his mind. Her confrontation with Isaac, her city's prince. That shit stain could die. Her internment. The warden. Dimitri's face and name were imprinted. That was another shit stain. He'd tasted her power and wanted it, that was why he'd brutalized her. Taken and taken until she'd nearly died, the last of her heartbeats so sluggish, she should have, and then he'd fed her blood.

Cupping her face, Alfred murmured, "You will have your vengeance, hellion. I give you my word."

Then he lifted her and carried her inside. Her heart beat so slow. Almost too slow. But he had time. He had to get her right to the very brink to break the last shadow chain. His brothers had done their best, but they didn't fully comprehend demons—or the fact that they tangled deeper than blood.

"Alfred," Fin called him as he passed by, striding toward the stairs to his own wing.

"Not now," he answered. Not while he had her on his tongue and in his mind. He saw every moment from her death to her awakening to her confrontations to when Maddox arrived in her cell.

The warden's visits were particularly colorful, and he planned to remove every inch of his taint. Of course, he'd known what she was, he couldn't have mistaken her for anything else. To control one like her would have given him enormous power.

"You drained her?" Maddox was in his way. The dragon's eyes furious, battle-readiness etched into his every muscle. Rogue stepped between them, but he couldn't contain the dragon's growl. "She wasn't ready for that."

"Later, Maddox," Alfred ordered him. "She's mine now."

His until he purged the taint, then his brothers could have at her again. The danger to them was more real than they'd realized. They'd done well to split her blood between them, to flush her with theirs. Smart.

The blood had sustained her. But the taint, no matter how minute, was still there.

Maddox lunged forward, and Rogue barely caught him. "Hold off," Rogue told him. "He's helping her."

"She's mine," Maddox challenged him, and the dragon's eyes were incensed. Cradling Fiona to him, Alfred met his stare and waited. The dragon was powerful. Had always been among one of the strongest creatures he'd ever encountered.

But he would fight his brother and his brother's fire if he demanded it. "I am not taking her from you forever," he told him. "You know this. Control yourself."

The dragon shuddered as he dropped his gaze to the woman in Alfred's arms and then up again. The mark on his throat drew Alfred like a laser.

"You bit her throat," Maddox snarled. "She doesn't want anyone at her throat."

He understood. "It was necessary."

"You scared her."

"I do not have time for this argument." Her heart grew more sluggish with each passing second. The brink of death drew closer. "I will speak to you all later." He nodded to Rogue, then continued.

Whatever debate occurred between the others, he tuned out. His focus was solely on the way her heart beat.

His rooms were open, a fire burning in the hearth and the bed made. The windows had been unshuttered, and everything aired out. Fresh furniture filled in the open spaces.

It was not the black coffin of Dimitri.

Satisfied with Rogue's choices, Alfred set her on the bed and then stripped away the robe that smelled of Fin and his brothers. Bite marks littered her chest. Two more on her thighs. They had been thorough in their choices.

Divesting his own clothes, he ignored the dust on them and then examined his skin. He needed a bath, but it would have to wait. He bit down on his wrist to get the blood flowing before he slid onto the bed and pulled her limp form into his lap. Her mouth opened as he drew his wrist closer, the scent of his blood rousing her.

When her heart beat stuttered and finally faded, only then did he press his wrist to her mouth. Maddox's roar punched through the near silence in the keep. Fin's mind reached out to him, but Alfred batted it away. Of the three, only Rogue didn't question him, yet his concern was there, a palpable force.

For all that he had held himself in reserve, the frost elf had already succumbed to the attraction. Hardly surprising, and Alfred wouldn't fight the need to be there. At first, nothing happened, but he waited as his blood trickled between her lips.

The silence. The absolute lack of a heartbeat.

Death hung like a curtain.

Then it shredded as she gripped his arm, and her mouth closed over the wound. The scrape of her teeth forced at his skin, trying to widen the slash. Stroking her hair away from her face, Alfred smiled down at her. "Feed, little hellion," he murmured. His whole body stirred to the contact with hers, but he focused on the gulps she took and the way color flushed across her breasts.

Life suffused her, and her scent curled around him until he wanted to sink his teeth into her again. But he had patience, he had to let her drain him, then he would drain her again.

More and more, she sucked, pulling harder, and his cock grew stiffer with every healthy pull. It defied logic, but then the idea that a mate existed for all four of them had always defied it.

When she fluttered open her lashes and looked up at him with near green eyes, Alfred smiled.

A queen.

Finally.

CHAPTER 15

"You have escaped the cage. Your wings are stretched out. Now fly."
- Rumi

*I*n its purest form, the act of retribution offered symmetry. It offered payment for a crime. The danger, however, was that retaliation often only furthered the cycle of violence. Yet, what else could I do when the greater offense would be to let a crime go unpunished?

Those thoughts filtered through my foggy brain as I roused to the taste of aged blood. The flavor was beyond anything I'd ever experienced. The effervescence of Fin, the spice of Maddox, and the cool fire of Rogue had become somewhat familiar to me. I wouldn't say I craved their blood, so much as I craved them.

This? The flavor sent spots of gold flickering like a flip-book of images played on fast forward. Intense aromas of brown sugar, toffee, and lime teased my palate as I rode horses, raced armies, faced the sun, and conquered my enemies. Battle and I were old friends, but I was always alone.

Others wanted to follow me, and I allowed it, but I never encouraged it. When Rogue came into my life, he had his own agenda. He fit, and when battle nearly took him, I saved his life. He did not thank me for it.

No, quite the opposite, he tried to kill me. It says something for our friendship that he tried to kill me for five years before he considered forgiving me.

He has been my friend ever since. My constant companion.

The images raced away, almost too fast for me to hold onto. I gasped when he pulled his wrist from my mouth and then tucked his face down to my throat.

"No," I tried to squirm, but his arms locked around me.

"Yes, my hellion. I am removing all trace of him from you." The rasp of his voice was a dark promise all its own, and my whole body seemed to go liquid. Then his teeth sank in, and I wanted to scream. Panic clawed its way up, but he didn't tear away or rend. His arms tightened, a hug not pinning me down, and with care, he began to stroke my hair.

I was in the shop. I loved this shop so much. We'd worked hard to cultivate the clientele. Mundane and supernatural, they all came to us. I didn't own the place, no, I just worked there, but I loved it. I loved the feeling infused into every part of the place.

"What's your favorite part?" The whisper of his voice against my ear had me turning. No one was there, but I looked to the wall of crystals. In the afternoon, when the sun hit them, it became a wall of light. Part of why my perfect house would be one with floor to ceiling windows where I could see the whole world, not some dark, cramped little apartment that faced the brick wall of the building next door.

"It's beautiful." Like a ghost, he trailed his fingers down my arm to take my hand. *"Show me your house?"*

It wasn't mine yet. Just a place. An idea.

"Show me." Command and request. Seduction and demand.

With a roll of my eyes, I retreated from the shop and walked out onto the deck of my cliff house. I could see it so perfectly. The salty air blew in from the west. The thrum of the waves a soothing soundtrack, even as birds called in the distance. He was indistinct, but he stood next to me as I leaned against the railing.

"Open...not very defensible."

I snorted. "I don't want to hide behind walls," I confessed. "I've lived in the shadows for so long. I want light. I want—this." Open skies. Open air. Light everywhere.

"Who kept you in the shadows, hellion?"

Life. What I was. Succubi didn't even want to be around their own kind. We separated from our families as soon as we could survive on our own. We dared not get too close. It was why I had to go.

"Shh...you don't have to do anything. Show me more."

I should tell him no. I really should. This was my place. I'd built it for me.

"Please."

The single word shocked me. I'd already wanted to show him, but now… Fine. I took his hand, threading my fingers with his, and guided him inside. The bedroom was exactly as I envisioned it. Huge, like the room I shared with Rogue, Maddox, and Fin. The bed was much bigger, too. So it was the same with a few tweaks.

He chuckled at the description as we moved toward the windows and looked out over the ocean. *"Magnificent."*

I thought so, too. It was why I wanted to be able to look

over it. Always. "Just imagine the sunset over the water…"
The light changed and played exactly as I'd wanted it to be.

"Show me more?"

The bathroom, the sunken tub and the oversized shower.
Though images of the pools in the bathing room flickered in
and out. Downstairs, I showed him the kitchen and dining
areas, but they were the library. Piece by piece, my house
turned into the keep and then changed back.

"It's all right, Fiona. Trust me."

Why should I? But he didn't answer the question as darkness crowded my vision, and then I was gasping as he lifted
his head. We were in some room I'd never been in before,
and Alfred gazed down at me, his lips red with my blood. He
rolled me over so I lay breast to chest, and then he tucked my
head to his throat. I knew what he wanted but I was so tired.

I didn't want to do this anymore.

"It hurts." It did. Everything hurt. Breathing hurt.

"You have almost no blood left," he told me as he stroked
the hair from my face. "It is like pulling poison from a
wound, Fiona. I have to cleanse it all, and I will cleanse it
through me."

That didn't even make sense.

"You must trust me."

"Why? You bit me."

He smiled. "And you may bite me, hellion."

I didn't even know him.

"Not true," he whispered, cradling my face when I
couldn't hold my own head up. My vision dimmed as my
heart slowed. Somewhere, a roar punched through the hum
in my ears.

Maddox.

"Will be fine. Fin and Rogue are with him. This is hard on
the dragon," Alfred warned me. "Don't fight me too long,
hellion, it hurts him."

I frowned. How was it hurting him? I didn't ask for this. I didn't ask for any of this.

"No," Alfred told me. "You didn't…now you must feed."

I hated him.

I hated all of them.

"I know," he soothed, rubbing my back as he nestled my face to his throat. The pound of his heart vibrated against my chest, and I licked at the skin. Just a trace of my tongue to gather the salt there, but it was far more decadent than salt, and I sank my teeth in. It took real effort to clamp down, and the hand on the back of my head urged me to keep going, even if it had to be hurting him.

The first gush of blood filled my mouth, and I closed my eyes, losing myself to the ecstasy. The pain receded as I drank.

Rogue led the way down the hillside. We had to move fast. The barbed spear fired by the ballista had hit the golden dragon's wing. It had crashed to the earth. There were so few of them left. If we didn't get there fast enough…

I had never moved so fast, only to seem like it wasn't fast enough. The dragon's heart thundered in my ears. Pain echoed in his roar, and the clash of steel reached us before we made it to the clearing, leaping the downed trees he'd ripped out as he tumbled from the sky.

Ahead of me by two steps, Rogue unleashed a deadly volley of ice daggers. They sliced right through the opponents, and I continued on. There were easier ways to kill, but I wanted to get to the dragon before further harm had been done to him. My blade cleaved through necks and severed heads. I was already on to the next before the first body fell.

The dragon's wing dragged the ground, the spear having torn the delicate membrane of the wing. He snapped and ripped one soldier in half with a chomp of his teeth and consumed the two past them with a flash of white-hot fire.

Their screams rent the air and then faded as they tumbled, burnt and blackened to the ground.

When the dragon swung his head to face me, I raised my hands, sword angled down. In my grip it was still dangerous, but my posture was non-threatening.

"I've come to help you," I told him. "You can kill me." Or try anyway. "Or you can let me free you. There are more of them coming. They've gotten very skilled at killing your kind."

The dragon glared, rage and pain radiated from him. The sound of running steps behind me had me twisting, and the head of the latest raider sailed from his shoulders as I stepped up to meet the assault. Rogue was soon at my side as we cut through the attackers.

When the last body dropped, I faced the dragon again. He'd been at our backs the whole time, and while he could have burned us, he hadn't. He stared steadily, and I passed the blade to Rogue.

"I am going to remove the spear," I informed him as I moved with purpose in his direction. "It won't heal as it is, and you won't be able to get off the ground."

Dragons were formidable creatures, but they were more vulnerable on the ground. The beast's pain beat at me. I could smell it in the air and feel it in the thunder of his pulse. When the dragon made no threatening move, I darted forward and gripped the spear. With a yank, it came free.

He roared, and my heart ached for him. I wanted to put a hand on him to help, but I had to move to avoid the snap of the damaged wing and the clack of his teeth coming together mere inches from my head.

Not a real attack. A warning.

"You're going to want to keep him, aren't you?" Rogue asked, his tone dry, and I shrugged.

In truth, I'd only wanted to help him. If he wanted to be a companion, I would not be opposed. "I think he likes me," I said with a grin, and Rogue laughed.

"I like you, didn't stop me from wanting to kill you."

This was true.

"Then you and he should get along well." I clapped Rogue on the shoulder. "Clean up the bodies, or leave them for him to eat?"

We eyed each other, then the dragon, who stared at us a moment. When he dipped his head to the bodies, I swore he smiled.

"Let him eat," Rogue agreed with me, and we withdrew to give him space.

Fingers in my hair tugged me away from his throat, and I met Alfred's dark gaze. Though his eyelids were half-lowered as though he was sleepy, I couldn't look away from the dangerous intensity housed there. The feeling of battle still surged in my veins, and the pleasure at saving such a magnificent beast.

Maddox.

He'd saved Maddox.

He'd saved Rogue, too. That was different in some ways. He'd saved Rogue for himself as much as for Rogue. But Maddox? He'd fought to get to him. Fought to keep him alive. Seeing him in the sun was so different from seeing him in the prison. He'd been majestic and proud. My heart wrenched to see him so hurt.

I licked my lips and then kissed Alfred. He let out a hum of approval as his tongue swept against mine. I lapped at the taste of my blood in his mouth while his coated mine. It was the strangest sensation and so absolutely right in the same breath.

The stroke of his hands along my sides had me arching,

his cock nestled against my labia, already slick from how wet I was, and I ground against him. His chuckle vibrated through me as he fisted my hair tighter, the tug lighting up my whole scalp. The desire eddied there, a constant thrum against my senses, but it wasn't hunger but true want. True need. I sucked against his tongue and dug my fingers into his shoulders.

When he rolled me over, I wrapped my legs around him, arching upward to tease along his thickening girth. Breaking the kiss, he nipped at my lower lip, and I groaned.

"Do you want this, hellion?" The question startled me. "Do you want *me*? Or are you responding to your hunger?"

Hurt struck like a slap, and I blinked. I wasn't hungry at all, but he was like holding onto a storm, all sizzling zaps to my senses, and he'd saved Maddox. I wanted…

"Shh," he shushed me with a nuzzling kiss that took him to my ear and then to my throat. "I have to know, because I will not take from you as the little coward did." The press of his lips ghosting over the marks he'd made had me shuddering. "I will wipe him from you, but you have to want me to be in my bed."

Wasn't I already in his bed? Despite my best efforts, the words wouldn't leave my tongue. The graze of his teeth had me clawing at his back as the panic bubbled up inside of me. Darkness edged my vision, and Alfred sighed.

Had I disappointed him? Fuck. Why did I care?

"When I get my hands on that demon, I'm going to have his entrails for garters." With that cryptic, if brutal statement, he bit me again, and this time I didn't pretend not to scream. It was like I was being burned from the inside out as he began to suck. The pleasure faded entirely to pain.

We were standing on the beach. The house was above, but I didn't look there, I kept my gaze on the water. "You keep killing me." It had taken me a moment to put it together, but the agony racing through my veins before clarified it.

"Yes," he told me. Well, at least he didn't sugarcoat it. "You don't want me to make it sweet."

I almost laughed. Twisting, I met his dark-eyed gaze. I really couldn't tell if his eyes were that dark because he was full of shit, or if his pupils had swallowed the irises. The corners of his mouth tipped up. "Why?"

"Because, Hellion…" He said the nickname like he had Fiona, and it sent a shudder through my whole system. "You fed on a shadow demon for weeks. You never fully transitioned. You basically slowed your own death, but death comes for everyone."

"So you're killing me? How does that logic work?"

"I'm turning you. I'm clearing away the stamp of the fool who tried to and the taint of the shadow demon who wanted to own you."

Anger flash-fired through me.

"Have no fear, Hellion. No one else will be able to claim you." He stroked a finger down my cheek.

"Except you."

"Except us," he corrected. "Fin is right. You do belong to us, but we also belong to you."

I rolled my eyes and jerked away from his touch. "I didn't ask any of you for this."

"I know."

"But you're doing it anyway."

"I can't let you die." The admission should make me feel something. Wanted. Needed. But all it made me feel was…

"That isn't *your* decision to make." I glared at him, and he gave me another of those faint smiles. It didn't quite reach his eyes though.

"It is very much my decision," he said. "As modern people are fond of saying, the buck stops here. I will make sure you have what is due you. The vengeance on those who harmed you."

"I can get that on my own."

"I have no doubt." At least he sounded like he meant that part. "Just as I have no doubt that I will very much enjoy helping you. The crimes done to you are numerous, and no one hurts what is mine."

I moved away from him, but I couldn't escape. He was there, like a shadow in my step. A pulse under my skin. He was pulling all the blood from my body.

Again.

"The pain is real," he murmured. "I can block most of it. But this is the best way to ease your transition."

"Wow, I'd hate to see the hard way."

He didn't comment. I focused on the ocean, on the foam of the sea as it rolled in and how the air tasted. I loved the ocean so much.

"Why?"

"What?"

"Why do you love the ocean?"

"Can you at least pretend to not read my mind?"

"Not right now, no," he said. "I am taking all of you into me, and then I am having you take me into you. You will know me as intimately as I know you when we are done."

Resentment sliced through me. "You turned Rogue without his permission."

"He hated me for a long time."

"Why did you do that?"

"Because he was my friend, and I did not want him to die."

"But he didn't want to live like this." Did Rogue and I have that in common? And I thought he was such an asshole to me.

"No," Alfred admitted, moving to stand next to me. I was

tempted to lean my head against his shoulder, but I resisted it.

Barely.

"He didn't think it natural. Elves are—they are very attuned to nature. He was—is a frost elf. He thrives in winter, it is his favorite season. His magic is a part of him. When I turned him, he lost some of that. He gained more, but...that took time for him to grieve and to acclimate."

"And you feel no regret for it." I dared him to lie to me. I'd been in that memory. I'd been there when he turned him.

"I do not regret saving my friend. Nor do I regret giving him the time to make his peace with it."

"Generous."

He shrugged.

The light faded, and it was getting darker. I sat abruptly. The sand was warm beneath me, even if the breeze was cold.

"I could just not drink."

"I cannot let you do that," he told me, and he sounded almost sorrowful. But he wasn't. He didn't regret doing this to Rogue, and now he wouldn't regret doing it to me.

"Did you force Fin, too?"

But even as I tried to focus on him, he faded. Through blurred vision, I found him hovering over me. His mouth was red with my blood. He pressed his lips to mine, a teasing kiss, and then ground his hips gently against me.

I refused. Even if my body wanted his, I refused.

I closed my eyes and blocked him out.

"Hellion," he whispered. "You have to drink. Take back from me what I have taken from you."

"No."

His sigh filled the room.

"Fiona," he commanded, and my name settled on me like strings attaching themselves and jerking me to move. I opened my eyes to find his throat right there. He rolled onto his back, pressing my face into his throat, and then he dragged a hand down to my ass, massaging it. "Drink."

I scraped my teeth against my lower lip. The pain had gone past the point I even cared about it. Breathing was hard, and my heart grew more sluggish. If I refused, if I turned away, this could all be over.

At the same time…

"Do you really want to die, Hellion?" Alfred squeezed my ass. "You'll take Maddox from us."

What?

I forced my tumbling eyes open.

"Possibly Fin, too."

I swallowed at my dry throat, and it burned. All I could smell was Alfred. His scent filled my nostrils, and I ached. Even as I told myself no, I began to roll my hips. His cock bumped against my clit, and a spear of pleasure darted through me. Licking at my dry lips, I tried to pull away, but he kept my face at his throat.

"Maddox has already let you claim him, Hellion—you're his mate. Do you hear his roars?" I had, though I'd tried to tune them out. The room seemed to vibrate from them. "He will tear this place apart to get to you if you do not drink."

I could almost hear him, pleading with me. *Drink, Kitten.*

You can hear him, Beautiful. Fin's voice slipped in. *You have to drink.*

I was so tired.

"You are almost done," Alfred promised. But that could be a lie. What did I know?

Beautiful, trust us. Please. You're ours. I asked you for time, and you said you would give it to us.

The tears in his voice threatened to gut me, and I squeezed my eyes shut. Maddox's roar thrummed through me, and I pressed my mouth down against Alfred's throat.

I hate you all.

A pause as I sank my teeth in, and that old blood rushed in to soothe all the pain. I clamped down faster this time, even as I sank down on his cock at once. The pleasure lit me up as his power flooded into me.

We know, Beautiful. Fin sounded so damn sad.

Then I heard nothing as I began to move, every thrust sending me higher as I drank, and Alfred stroked me through it. When his memories swam up to swallow me, I fought them off, focusing on the way he stretched me and how my nipples scraped against his chest.

I drank until he went lax beneath me and came with a shout, my own orgasm staggering me.

Then and only then did I lift my head.

Meeting his gaze, I waited. His cock was still buried deep, and his eyes gleamed. "Yes?" he demanded.

And I finally understood the question.

He offered me himself, but I had to give in return. I had to give willingly.

Fine, if that was the only way out of this prison—the only way to be strong enough to defeat them all—then I'd take it.

"Yes."

Pleasure flared in his eyes, and Maddox's roar changed. Fin brushed his thoughts to mine, his regret and triumph tangled too tightly together for me to separate. Then they all faded. The only one I didn't feel or see was Rogue. Perhaps he understood my decision best of all.

Alfred gripped my hair and flipped me over, then struck.

As his teeth pierced me, I surrendered.

It looked like I was going to be a damn vampire after all.

Fiona may have surrendered this battle, but the war has only

begun. Alfred, Rogue, Maddox, and Fin will have their hands full when we return in
Succubus Unchained.
To keep up with Heather and all her series join her reader's group:
https://www.facebook.com/groups/HeathersPack/

ABOUT HEATHER LONG

USA Today bestselling author, Heather Long, likes long walks in the park, science fiction, superheroes, Marines, and men who aren't douche bags. Her books are filled with heroes and heroines tangled in romance as hot as Texas summertime. From paranormal historical westerns to contemporary military romance, Heather might switch genres, but one thing is true in all of her stories—her characters drive the books. When she's not wrangling her menagerie of animals, she devotes her time to family and friends she considers family. She believes if you like your heroes so real you could lick the grit off their chest, and your heroines so likable, you're sure you've been friends with women just like them, you'll enjoy her worlds as much as she does.

Follow Heather & Sign up for her newsletter:
www.heatherlong.net

The Quick & The Fevered

A Man Called Wyatt

Going Royal

Some Like It Royal

Some Like It Scandalous

Some Like It Deadly

Some Like it Secret

Some Like it Easy

Her Marine Prince

Blocked

Heart of the Nebula

Queenmaker

Deal Breaker

Throne Taker

Lone Star Leathernecks

Semper Fi Cowboy

As You Were, Cowboy

Madison, The Witch Hunter

Every Witch Way But Floosey's

Magic & Mayhem

The Witch Singer

Bridget's Witch's Diary

The Witched Away Bride

Mongrels

Mongrels, Mischief & Mayhem

Shackled Souls
Succubus Chained
Succubus Unchained

Space Cowboy
Space Cowboy Survival Guide

Special Forces & Brotherhood Protectors
Securing Arizona
Chasing Katie
Guarding Gertrude
Protecting Pilar
Wrangling Wanda
Shielding Shayna
Covering Coco
Hijacking Holiday

Untouchable
Rules and Roses
Changes and Chocolates
Keys and Kisses
Whispers and Wishes

Wolves of Willow Bend

Wolf at Law
Wolf Bite
Caged Wolf
Wolf Claim

Wolf Next Door

Rogue Wolf

Bayou Wolf

Untamed Wolf

Wolf with Benefits

River Wolf

Single Wicked Wolf

Desert Wolf

Snow Wolf

Wolf on Board

Holly Jolly Wolf

Shadow Wolf

His Moonstruck Wolf

Thunder Wolf

Ghost Wolf

Outlaw Wolves

Wolf Unleashed

Spirit Wolf

Printed in Great Britain
by Amazon